Tell Me I'm Wrong

Michelle K. Blanchard

Printed in the United States of America
First Printing, 2019, Second Printing 2020
Print ISBN 978-1-7324619-4-9
E-Book ISBN 978-1-7324619-5-6
www.facebook.com/michelleblanchardauthor
Cover art by baytunc at iStock by Getty Images ©

I dedicate this book to you. The reader.

The one taking a chance on a new author. Thank you.

To those who have found your love, found and lost your love or still waiting for your love.

1

Cole

"Evans, No!!!"

"Evans, you asshole!"

"We are under fire! Tommy's hit!"

I scream into the radio, dropping my equipment on the ground. I follow Stafford into the thick brush trying to seek cover. I walk with heavy feet as my friend lay lifeless across my shoulders. Tommy's head wound drips with blood which pools at the tips of his fingers. His hand flops with the pace of my steps leaving a spotty trail of blood on the dirt road.

The sweat and dirt muddy my eyelids, obstructing my sight. In between struggled breaths, I choke on the dry Iraqi dust.

I clear it and spit. I cough and spit again.

Blood.

"Shit. Stafford, where's cover? Staff—Rhett?"

Rhett turns and his face has a look of horror. His eyes widen involuntarily as his chest explodes with enemy fire; barely audible he murmurs his last words.

"Run…Cole."

***

I wake. I sit up violently, coughing, and screaming; sweating profusely as I run my fingers through my damp hair. I know he's not here, but I look around for Rhett anyway. I cup my left shoulder and run my finger across the scar to be sure the bullet isn't still there, a forever reminder of that day. Two of my best friends, gone.

I tear the covers off exposing every part of my skin, hoping it'll help steady my breathing. The nightmare is always the same.

It's early and tearing the covers off has pushed fine dust particles into the air, an all too familiar sight from overseas. I struggle to my feet and sit motionless on edge of the bed. My eyes adjust to the sun breaking through the ripped curtain. The Autumn breeze whistles through the crack in the window drawing my attention to it. I stare at it emotionless. Paige would nag me about needing to replace that window every time she cleaned it.

"Colton, it has a crack the size of the Grand Canyon," she'd say.

Except for the last ten minutes when my nightmare started, I didn't sleep all fucking night. I look around orientating myself to my surroundings. I rub my sore eyes pushing a little harder than I should as if trying to shove away the sights and sounds that continuously torment me.

My dresser is covered with clean clothes, and if I'm honest, probably some dirty ones too. They never make it into drawers, not anymore. That one chore Paige did for me is now hard evidence that she's gone. There are no pictures hanging on the wall, her half of the closet is empty, and her nightstand bare. Clothes hangers are scattered across the carpet as if she left in a hurry. There is very little left to remind me of Paige. She took everything and left me with nothing.

"Shit." I sigh and release my breath, still rubbing my eyes as I exit my bedroom.

I fear the stillness and silence that lies behind my bedroom door, so I pace slowly to the bathroom trying to stall the inevitable.

I don't hesitate stepping into the shower before the water turns warm. The dinner plate shower head spits cold water like daggers. The tiny prickles distract me from my fucking life for ten to fifteen seconds. I lather the shampoo into my hair, wash my body, and curse in frustration when my hand presses over my left shoulder. I stand and wait, and once the cold-water returns, I know my shower is over.

My bathroom is beautiful if I say so myself. Dustin and I did a nice job modernizing it when I bought the place. Paige *had* to have his and her double sinks and the huge spa tub to match. She loved the idea of being surrounded by water when she showered, so I sprung for a dinner plate-sized shower head. But it was always her long hot baths which she loved the most. There were plenty of times I'd find her soaking the black Jacuzzi tub, cocooned by gray walls, accent towels, and candlelight. Always, with a glass of wine in hand, saying it was her escape.

I'm brought back to the present, faltering only for a moment when I see the gaping hole in the wall. As my towel falls off hitting the hallway floor, I stand stark naked as I recall the night my fist went through that wall.

Four months ago, almost to the day, the night I got home from my last tour; my *final* tour, the end of my military career. I had found my girl and she and I were to be married. A diamond ring and a "yes" promised me hope for a future with her. I had been planning the day with Dustin for a while. I was coming home to surprise her, and we would finally start our life together, maybe even a family. Paige, however, had other plans, and those plans didn't include me. I got home a day too early and I walked in on *my* girl being fucked by some asshole. Well, I should say she was doing the fucking. When I found them, she was gyrating on top of his dick. His hands were cupped over her breasts and her head was thrown back in what appeared to be pure pleasure. Knowing the intensity of her moans were originating from another man's touch severed me in two.

I stand there in the hallway numb, as I recall her betrayal, and it only rubs salt in the wounds after this morning's nightmare. In a fit of rage and before I know what I'm doing, I supply the wall with another hole; one that rivals the first.

Angrily I sift through the pile of clothes on the dresser.

"God damn it." I curse annoyingly as I finally find myself clean socks and boxers.

Hanging neatly pressed in the closet, my uniform awaits me. Ironing it seems to be the only thing I can keep organized anymore.

I push my wallet into my back pocket. Wrap my belt around my waist, secure my cuffs, and clip in my firearm. I snag my keys on a throw –I like the sound it makes.

Making my way to the kitchen, I realize it lacks the smell of freshly brewed coffee. Paige knew how to start my day and she'd have breakfast prepared each morning.

"It's scary enough watching you leave let alone leave on an empty stomach, now eat." She used to say.

I look over the kitchen making sure I've not forgotten anything and head for the door, passing the couch where Paige and I made love numerous times. Afterwards, we'd sit up until the early morning hours planning our next fifty years together. She's supposed to be here. We are supposed to be together.

Before leaving my apartment, my eyes fly up to the deer head mounted over the fireplace, courtesy of my brother. Paige hated it.

"I feel like he's always watching us bang," she'd say.

The waterworks can't be helped; the bareness of the apartment reminds me that she's still gone.

***

"*It's Cole*," I greet as I close my pickup truck door.

"*I'm on my way Captain. Yes, all the details are in the report.*" I roll my eyes humorously, "*yes, yes…it's on your desk, Pop.*"

My father has been with the police department for forty-one years. I used to run around the hallways while he brought in the bad guys. I'd gawk at and follow them around, pulling out my plastic cowboy gun, pretending to shoot them when they weren't looking. Pop would never let me see the jail cells. But he would joke about how—at the rate my brother, Dustin, and I were going, we'd see them one day. Now, being an officer at my father's precinct, I do see them every day.

I turn the ignition, roll the window down, and turn up the CCR song. I peel out with my usual mission and that's to grab coffee on the way to the PD.

***

"You're late." Pop welcomes me tersely as I attempt to quietly enter the room.

"Oh, Cap you know as well as I that we can't start our day without coffee and a donut." I toss him the brown paper bag which is now appearing wet from the greasy pastry. I make my way to the back of the room and find my seat, throwing a few shoulder punches, and slaps to the back of heads as my buddy's chuckle mockingly.

"Thanks, son. We're just going over today's briefing."

"Ah, you still have me on patrol?" I shout out to him *not* jokingly as I take my seat.

"Until your mother says otherwise, yes." He quips.

Laughs intensify from the guys.

"Eh, ease up assholes. You wish you had a mama as sweet as mine."

Without hesitation Pop controls the room, and in all the seriousness he can muster spends the remainder of the report refreshing the deputies on the Olden shooting.

"Again ladies, a 10-71 over on South Campbell Road, the home of Brad and Angel Olden. 911 was dispatched after shots were fired at the residence. What's unclear is how Mrs. Olden ended up on the ground from a

gunshot wound. Intentional or accidental, who the hell knows? I sure as hell don't."

The room stirs in response to my father's exasperated tone. I stand to interject offering my father who's pushing sixty-seven a breather.

"When I arrived, Dave and the EMS were tending to Mrs. Olden. The Olden's aren't talking yet so it's making it very difficult to proceed. We don't have a make of the vehicle, a description of this jackass, frankly we have no leads.

The room erupts in chatter.

Pop raises his voice over the commotion to finish the briefing.

"Ladies, I don't care what else is going on today, find me a lead on the car, the shooter, the bullet in Mrs. Olden, something, and Cole, patrol."

I didn't need the reminder.

***

"I swear if I'm not a fucking cliché," I mutter to myself as I sit in the patrol car drinking hot coffee and eating one of Pop's left-over grease bombs.

I have the music loud enough to hear the song playing but low enough to hear the calls coming in over the police radio.

Traffic duty in Lorry Springs is boring as fuck. It's a good size town with quaint shops and unique cafes and it has a southern country feel, but not a lot of action happens here. Routine calls, minor fender-benders, people running red lights, and a few idiots trying their hand at a misdemeanor or two. But when there's action like the Olden shooting, Lorry Springs makes the headlines and the last place I want to be is in a patrol car. I'm an investigator for gods' sakes, not a first-year rookie.

I push the last of the donut into my mouth. I look down to find crumbs on my shirt which I brush off and onto the car floor. My eye-roll is automatic as my inner self calls me a slob. I lift my coffee out of its holder and give it a blow, like *that'll* do anything to prevent it from burning my mouth.

I hate patrol. It offers too much time to think, to remember, to dwell on the past and what was going to be my future. A perfect future with Paige until I found her perfect legs parted wide for some asshole. Four months is plenty of time to get over someone, right? Truth be told, it is over the second my mind registered what was playing out in front of me. I had turned around and walked out on her before they saw me. Leaving a simple and clear message for her to find the fucking door and wander through it. It must have spoken volumes because she was gone by the time my shift ended the following day. That hole is the only real reminder I have that I had any emotional reaction to her cheating. If I'm honest, I'm not sure if I miss her or the idea of her at this point. Early on yes, I missed everything about her, how she smelled, how cute her laugh was, and I missed all the little things she'd do for me.

I force the thought of her out of my mind, blow on my coffee, and take another tentative sip.

It's going to be a long fucking day.

***

Without warning the hair on my arms spring to life as the screech of rubber on pavement rings joyously in my ears. My respite is about to show itself.

I sit up and adjust my ass in the seat. My nerves begin to bite, and my heart starts hammering. My hand develops a steady tremor as it does when my adrenaline starts flowing. Without taking my eyes off the highway, I slowly secure my coffee back into its holder.

I'm ready.

I wait.

I watch like a predator watches its prey.

2

Mya

"I don't have time for this!" I whisper to myself panicking as I watch the rear-view mirror.

The police car pulls out behind me with its red and blue lights circling fast, the siren screaming and demanding for me to respond.

"Shit, shit—shit." I pull over.

My already panicked state is heightened even more as I sit idle. Keeping an eye on the rearview mirror, just past the police car hoping I don't see *him*.

An hour, that's all I wanted with Trisha to tell her what happened. I didn't get two words out before he walked in. I was with Trisha, yes, but it didn't keep my hands from shaking or my stomach from turning. It's been years, but I knew it was him. It seems being in the same place as him still rattles me. With one look, I remember all the times he'd struck me and the bruises he'd leave behind. It took me a long time to move past the wounds Peter left me with.

"Mya, what has your panties in a twist?"

Trisha pulled my attention back to Pins. A small diner in the middle of town with vintage tables and décor. Behind the frilly drapes there's a 1950's spa where you can get your hair and nails done. There's even a patio with an outdoor fire pit. I love it here. The waitresses dress like pinup girls all the while keeping the floozy look to a minimum. The coffee is delish, and the pastries are fattening. Trisha and I only come here when we have some serious girl-talk to discuss. Afterwards, I usually head straight to the gym.

"Mya." She tried again to collect my attention and she succeeded. Now wide-eyed and commenting on how ghost white I appeared her attempts to calm me failed. I shot up from my seat drawing the attention of other patrons in the diner, including *him*. I left Pins, got in my white two door coupe and sped away, but not before making a scene.

One corner and a tire wheel squeal later, and here I am.

***

"What the hell is taking him so long? Come give me my ticket and let's get this show on the road," I complain to myself.

In the side view mirror, I see the police car door open. With my eyes glued to the mirror, I suddenly forget about the drama I left back at Pins. My fingers tap rapidly on the steering wheel as I pray this moment to be over soon.

I hear his heavy footsteps long before I see him. His boots pounding the pavement, now in sync with my heartbeat. The closer he gets the less view I have of him, but his walk alone has my heart pumping fast. The most perfect strut I've ever seen approaches my driver-side window. An intoxicating smell slams into my nose, my mind swirls with lustful thoughts, and the delicious pulse throbbing in my lady parts requires my attention.

"Ma'am." He says tipping his fancy cowboy police hat.

"Do you know why I pulled you over today?"

That voice. That deep, husky voice sends shivers down my spine making my nipples stiffen. I gaze up at him just as he removes his sunglasses. His sea blue eyes begin to penetrate every layer of my subconscious. His gaze calms my fears and settles my nerves and for another moment I forget who I was running from.

His blond hair peeks out from under his patrol hat and a sharp jawline surrounds his full lips. He's built; I can see his toned frame hammering through his shirt. The smell of leather rivals his cologne and the sounds alone make me dizzy. As his hips sway in front of me, he leverages his hand on his belt, white knuckled in front of his gun, ready to make a quick move if he must. A hint of an arm tattoo sweetens the deal as he stands there all "Officer Sex on Legs." With his lips slightly parted, he glares down at me still waiting for my response.

"I was, I am, in a hurry," I press tersely but I get no reaction out of him. I smile sweetly to see if I can move this along. He's still not impressed.

"Ma'am, I clocked you doing 50 after peeling out from the corner over there," he nods as if pointing with his eyes behind us, forcing me to match his direction. An upsurge of nausea whitens my face when I see another vehicle has also pulled off to the side of the road.

"The limit's 30, Miss," he continues, but pauses briefly as I bring my eyes back to his. My paranoia silences my voice and the officer takes notice.

"Can I see your license and registration, please?" His tone has shifted. He's concerned.

With a shaky hand, I give him both. He takes the documents, lightly grazing my hand with his fingertips as he does. My senses spark to life and I pull away quickly as if his touch just electrocuted me.

"Just a moment, Miss. Sit tight," he states tentatively as he examines the area behind his car, but it doesn't matter, the vehicle pulls away just as he reaches his car door.

I begin deep breathing, one of my favorite coping skills courtesy of years in therapy. Several minutes go by. I settle down relieved there's a policeman nearby, so I release my held breath.

I look in the rearview mirror to check my complexion, makeup, and hair. I hear the car door shut and I know *Officer Sex on Legs* is on his way back to me. He startles me when he leans just inside the window of my coupe. His forearms resting securely on my window. The intoxicating smell of cologne and leather invade my nose again. He's only inches from my face and his three-day stubble is screaming for me to touch it.

"Please slow down, Miss. Is there anything else I can help you with today?"

Oh, that voice. My stomach swarms with butterflies as I start a pipedream. You mean like, take me home, wrap me in those tattooed arms and fuck me unconscious?

I fantasize silently but respond abruptly, and with a hint of an attitude with, *"No, I'm all set."*

I speed off, anxious to get to where I was going to in the first place.

3

Cole

I'm greeted with pats on the back and weak punches to the gut as the weekend deputies bullshit with me, asking me how many donuts I ate today.

"Yeah, yeah, enjoy your naps this weekend fellas since I caught all the little fuckers today." I bullshit back.

Officers at the Lorry Springs PD are closer than brothers, some of us are brothers. Regardless of what kind of mess we find ourselves in, we always have each other's back. At the end of most shifts and especially for those who have no one to go home to we flock to Styne's. The Tavern I bought a few years ago where Dave and I play every Friday night.

"Dustin, see you tonight at Styne's?" 8 o'clock?" I yell to my brother across the locker room. I get only a speechless nod as confirmation in return. He's chatting on the phone with I assume his latest love interest. I think the last one lasted about a month, the one before that, maybe three months. If his current interest doesn't become *interesting* soon, he'll be moving on.

When he turns non-verbal, I know he's about had it and he's biting his tongue before he lashes out over something stupid. My brother is a free spirit, but he seems to only attract women who want to settle down with 6 kids and a mortgage. When he's not working, he's traveling, camping or jumping out of airplanes in some exotic country.

I smile and rub my eyes as if I'm a crying baby. He gives me a *fuck you* through terse lips, a roll of the middle finger and a brotherly nod.

I drop the last of today's files on the patrol desk. One slips out of my hand and lands at my feet. *Mya Dylan, speeding, 50 in a 30*, I read as I recall the woman in the white coupe. A beautiful but shaken woman. Her soft brown curls swept over her shoulders every time she'd look away from me.   Quite possibly midweek masturbation material, but then the ballsy girl had the nerve to spin out on me when I let her go.

I notice her address as I pick up the file from the floor. North Campbell Road. How did I miss that? I tuck the address away, scribble on the file, and drop it on top of the others.

I pull out toward Styne's calling it a day.

4

Mya

"*Are you ready, yet?*" Trisha yells to me from my living room.

"*Almost. It takes time to make this shit beautiful,*" I holler back, knowing she's in a huff over not being at Styne's yet.

Trisha is my red headed, green eyed, wild girl bestie, with legs and abs that would make any model envious. She makes most men drool, and hell, I'm jealous of her adorable freckled pale skin.

She's trying her best to get me out of the house, so I go easy on her. After an abusive relationship and a failed fresh attempt at "getting back out there," she's determined to show me there's still great men to be had.

"*Okay, ready*," I say walking out from my bedroom having finally decided on something to wear. I wave my hand up and down my front wordlessly, asking if I made the right choice with my outfit.

"*It's perfect,*" Trisha confirms, as she looks over my pale-yellow sundress, jean jacket, and cowboy boot-hat ensemble. "*Nice touch.*" She giggles as she points to the white lace socks peeking over the top of my brown leather boots.

"*You think? I didn't know what to wear to this he-haw place you're taking me to.*"

"*Oh please, you love drinking—dancing, you love country—rock...hum country rock,*" she giggles, and I roll my eyes admiring her attempt at a joke.

"*You're going to love it and you look hot. And Oh My God*" –as if she forgot— "*you must tell me what the hell happened earlier. You shot out of Pins like a bullet and I haven't heard from you since, well until right now obviously.*" She chuckles, pausing her movements to turn toward me.

I freeze instantly knowing her dagger-like eyes are waiting for me to explain myself. My mind struggles for something to tell her. *"It was nothing. I thought I saw Evan. I haven't spoken to him since we broke up and I just didn't want to run into him."*

My paranoia fit from earlier has passed and as expected all is back to normal with me. As I promised her a long time ago, I didn't mention Peter's name. Though she's mostly only heard the stories from that time of my life, she's set on never hearing his name again. I suppose it's her way of protecting me or encouraging me move on. So that's what I'm doing. Whomever was in that vehicle, clearly does not involve me. It was just a random car with a random person in it, I can't always be so paranoid. If Peter saw me at Pins earlier, he would have reached out to me by now, right? Maybe I'm unrecognizable, it has been a few years after all.

I peek over and spot the curious look on Trisha's face, but I think I sold it. It's a weak excuse, but she's back fluffing her hair and applying her lip gloss, so I settle in for the win. I decide I won't go into details about my speeding ticket or the super-hot cop that pulled me over, even though she'd go doe-eyed over the tale. It'll only lead to questions about why I was speeding, and it *wasn't* because of Evan.

"Let's get out of here, I'm thirsty," she exclaims. She spins away from the mirror; her straight red hair sprays

out away from her like a 50's poodle skirt. She's out the door in a flash and I follow.

***

Our uber pulls up outside the tavern. Styne's Tavern is a beautiful cabin, lifted high on enormous stone pillars overlooking the mountains and the city lights. Thick, dark, parallel logs span the front of the cabin with tall vertical trunks stabilizing a deep wrap-around porch. The front peaks cascade down with glass. The view must be amazing from those windows, where the soft light is being carried from room to room. Huge mums sway from the porch roof with other Autumn decorations sprinkled throughout. The place is buzzing with people outside and in. We exit the car and my smile widens as the music can now be heard from outside the uber. It sounds like a live band inside. It's charming.

"Trisha, this place is amazing." I call out after her.

"It's an FGL cover!" Trisha screams excitedly over the music and chatter as we climb the steps to the vast wrap-around porch.

As we enter the double doors, we walk into what could be called an oversized mud room. We check our coats and continue through a set of swinging saloon doors, the kind that you'd see in an old western movie. The place is littered with people drinking, dancing, and

28

socializing. Some are making out in the corner where there's a spread of couches.

We make our way through the crowd. I look around taking in the enormity of the room with its high ceiling rafters and wooden beams. A spacious balcony wraps around the room and overlooks the dance floor. You could watch everything happening in the bar from up there. The rusty light fixtures hang from the beams offering just enough light for ambiance. There are cowboy memorabilia everywhere; the place screams country, and I immediately fall in love. Eventually we arrive at the bar where beers and shots are already waiting for us.

"Ladies. Courtesy of the gentleman down the bar," the elderly bartender rumbles with a grin pointing in the direction of a man sitting comfortably alone. Almost in unison we say thank you and glance down to the cowboy who looks like he's just stepped out of last year's calendar. His perfect body planted firmly on the barstool as if he owns it. His muscular arms crossed in front of him. His cowboy hat dipped low and his jawline cleanly shaven.

"He's hot, he's a cowboy, and he's all mine," Trisha squeals eagerly into my ear. I roll my eyes and laugh. Trisha is such a flirt. She dates a lot but has yet to find the perfect match to her wild lifestyle. We decide to have the fun we set out to have tonight. On a combined giggle, we throw our shots back and slam the glasses

down on the bar top. She scoops up her beer and dashes away in the cowboy's direction.

I laugh over my drink, watching as my assertive friend disappears toward her fling for tonight. I pick out my stool, lean back against the bar, and watch the band, who is now covering a Luke Bryan song. The tall one stands behind his guitar moving his body in rhythm. I can tell he really likes what he does, and he positively has eyes for the lead female singer. The drummer is cute. His chubby belly bounces with each hit as he beats away on the drums.

It's the second guitar player though that my body is responding to. His eyes are fixed on me. His gaze unwavering, and it seems he's singing directly to me. I fix my hair nervously, tucking a loose tendril behind my ear. I'm sure all the women in here are thinking the same thing should he glance in their direction. I feel my face flush as I sheepishly turn myself away, sure it's my imagination.

A glimpse, just one more small glance at him. Before long, my eyes are drawn to his fingers strumming the guitar. The guitar cradles his lap perfectly. I imagine myself there instead and all my muscles tighten. His singing voice is husky, deep, and beautiful. Perfect for country music. His short blond hair has a shallow wave on top.   His lips are full, and his smile intensifies the twists already in my belly and deepening the ache between my thighs. I take him all in, every inch of his exposed skin, wondering what he might smell like. He notices my observation of him, and he cracks a crooked grin in between lyrics as if to confirm *yes,* he *is* looking at *me.*

I literally just ended a relationship and I'm certainly not looking to get into another one. Acknowledging my self-revelation, I force my eyes to turn away. I spin my ass around slowly, trying not to be obvious about my fake disinterest. I look over to check on Trisha and she and her new-found cowboy are chatting, laughing, and falling all over each other. Well, she's falling all over him; he has his arms spread across the back of the booth as not to inappropriately touch her in her tipsy condition. But his gaze is locked on her smile and his eyes in awe of her.

I decide there is no time like the present to drink to this week's drama. I take my attention off Trisha. I finish my beer in a swift gulp and signal the bartender for another.

For a second time, I instinctively turn on my stool as if there is an invisible force that is willing me to do so. I find myself watching him again. Occasionally our gazes lock and I feel as though there's something familiar about him or at least how steady I feel when he's looking at me.

The dance floor obstructs my view at times, but when he does catch my eye, it's like everyone else disappears.

He looks delicious, the epitome of a cowboy. His faded jeans hug his thighs and his gray t-shirt is haphazardly tucked in on one side. He has a red and tan flannel on, and his sleeves are rolled up to his elbows. His cowboy hat, now on, casts a mysterious shadow across his face. We exchange playful smiles and his singing voice has my stomach doing cartwheels. It's been a while since a man touched me in a way that made me feel this alive, but this cowboys eyes alone has me shivering with pleasure. I watch his fingers dance effortlessly across the guitar. I begin daydreaming about what those fingers could do to me. The thought alone causes liquid warmth to pool between my thighs.

I feel hot; I unknowingly start fanning myself with the pub's menu and signal the old man to bring me another drink. I roll my eyes at my ridiculous reaction to this guy, wishing there was another distraction other than the one on stage.

5

Cole

The best place in the world for me is behind this guitar. I love singing and feeling the energy of the room. My parents bought me my first guitar when I was six. I taught myself how to play and have been strumming it ever since. It's where I feel most free from my troubles, it's my time to let go, and release the stress that builds day after day. Every Friday night, Dave, Nan, and I sing, and people watch, and have a good fucking time.

I can barely remember my lyrics when she walks in. I recognize her immediately; she's in *my* bar. I watch as she takes it in, pointing and smiling, looking around with admiration. My heart starts racing as I take in her features, *again*. She's tall and slender. She turns slowly showing off her profile; god, she's gorgeous. I fumble on the guitar and she glances toward the band in response none-the-wiser as she's grinning from ear to ear.

My memory quickly recounts today's traffic stop. I remember her fearful eyes and the hurried scans in her rearview mirror. None of it sat well with me. She seemed frightened and I felt an instinctual need to protect her. Like any good cop who sensed something was off, I tried to find out what I would be protecting her from, but she did not offer anything more when I asked if there was anything else, I could do. When I ran her license, I learned it was her first ticket, so I chalked her odd behavior up to nerves.

The sexiest laugh pulls me from my recollection and has my cock pressing against my Wranglers. Her wavy brown hair cascades down from her shoulders to the top of her ass. An ass that is barely covered by the hem of her dress. She maintains her modesty with a jean jacket which barely covers her front, and her necklace pools in between her breasts. I'm envious of that necklace but my eyes drop to her boots. Fuck, I love a woman in boots. She turns again, and I see the most delicate smile. I watch in awe as she talks with her friend. She forms each word slowly and with care, her tongue leaving her mouth every so often to moisten her lips. I want to taste those lips. I'm only slightly annoyed when I see my brother has already supplied her with a drink. All annoyances gone though, when her friend darts in Dustin's direction leaving *my* girl alone for the taking.

"Get a grip, Cole, Jesus," I utter to myself as Nan finishes her line.

My singing is a bit huskier with my nerves shattered about. Being in the same room with her has completely muddled my mind. I'm having a physical reaction to her appearance, to her laugh, and to those fucking boots.

I find myself staring again, singing softly as if I'm singing directly to her. She thinks I'm not looking at her, but I am, and she returns a timid grin and blushes. It's a routine we've quickly adopted. I mentally give myself a pep talk and through the lyrics, I smile all the while trying to keep my shit together. It's good to see her smile, which is quite the opposite from the last time I saw Mya Dylan.

***

The DJ comes to offer the band a break. I prop my guitar in its stand, straighten out my hat, and make my way to the bar. Women tug and pull at me for a hug or a brief kiss on the cheek, but I politely push past them, never taking my eyes off *her*. My eyes are fixed on Mya, and her slim, delicate figure. It seems to take an eternity to reach her. For fear of not getting to her in time I hurry my last few steps.

"Pay that speeding ticket yet?" I ask coolly over her shoulder steadying myself with one hand on the bar top.

She turns slowly, smirking over her beer. I match her beam with my own as I accept the beer being handed to me from Wyatt.

I'm within a foot of her; I can smell her peach shampoo. Her hair looks like silk, her skin tan and soft, and those fucking boots cry for my hand to touch the lace peering over the top. I stare at her mouth and find myself daydreaming about licking her pouty lips and being able to taste the beer she's drinking. It's all I can do to not go primal, bend her over this bar, and fuck her until she screams.

"Well, if it isn't Officer Sex on Legs," she states playfully. I choke on a laugh as if she's just heard my thoughts.

"I've been called worse," I reply, clearing my throat and tipping my hat to hide my true intentions.

I sit my ass down on a barstool next to her, trying to tame the erection I feel growing. She turns so her knees are between my legs and her full front is facing me. Her breasts are perky and present, ricocheting pulses directly to my cock. Her eyes begin taking me in. First my jeans, then my gray t-shirt behind my open flannel. She makes her way up my frame and I grin purposely when her eyes land on my mouth. Her green eyes scream with want, and I'm getting hard as fucking hell just watching her inspection of me.

"First time in my bar?" I ask, keeping the pace for fear of silence.

"Your bar?" She coughs but cheekily continues. *"My friend dragged me out. Shit week."* She takes a sip of her beer behind a devilish smirk. *"After being pulled over for speeding and all."* She's tipsy and she's being coy.

"Ah...that is shitty." I'll play along. She remembers me and the booze has us relaxed enough to play this game.

"They say if you go to court and the officer doesn't show...the Judge will let you out of a fine." She's mocking me; stifling a laugh as her perfect lips form for another drink.

"Oh, I'm sure he'll show." I respond, but I can barely get the words out. My attention is on her puckered lips wrapping around the head of the bottle.

"Oh," she counters, smirking as her tongue slips slightly into the glass hole as if directing the amber liquid into her mouth.

"Fairly certain, he might not ever see you again otherwise." I gaze at her wondering if I just crossed a line, but her eyes tell me something completely different. I lean in, closing the distance between us. I let a rogue curl slip through my fingers as I bring my fingertips across her cheek to her lips. I trace her bottom lip encouraging her to open them *"...and I want see you*—I lower myself and growl just above a whisper into her ear—*when I make you come."*

She pulls away tentatively and lowers her head, I see her cheeks billow, she's smiling. I lift her chin in hopes of finding her eyes, hoping still I didn't earn myself a slap.

She doesn't give me her eyes, instead, behind her subtle grin, she begins to breathe more heavily. She stands and takes a step into me, grazing her knee against my cock. She trails her hand up my arm and wraps it around my bicep. Slowly she walks her fingers down my arm pulling the sleeve up revealing my tattoo.

"Military?" She asks softly.

"Marines."

"That's hot." She continues to trace a single finger down to my hand bringing my whole body to goosebumps. Her touch is my undoing.

"Cop. Cowboy. Marine. Do you have any other secret identities?" she hums as she intertwines her fingers with mine, pushing her breasts in my frame.

Well, fuck. That just tipped me over the edge.

"Come here." I command firmly as I stand to my feet. My tall frame swallows her, causing her to step back. She's gorgeous and a flirt and my cock can't take anymore. She's doing things to me I don't comprehend.

I grab her by the hand, round the bar, and I take her into the hallway, away from the crowds. I push her against the supply closet door and kiss her hard and deep. The sound of liquid fizzling on the floor tells me she still has a beer in hand.

Her other hand quickly falls and through my jeans she rubs my cock which is now bulging and demanding to be released. I'm trying to match her urgency; but her pace is fast and commanding. I lean down and grab the bottom of her dress and slide my hand underneath until she releases a moan into my mouth. Her pleasurable sigh tells me I've touched the right spot and her pace slows almost willing the sensations to last longer. Her underwear is already wet, and I crave sinking my fingers deep inside her, but I won't, not now. I pull my hand away, release her, and take a step back. Taking a beat, I force my body into the opposite wall, but her body follows mine as if there is a magnetic lure keeping us together.

"Not tonight," I tell her as I take the beer from her hand, suggesting she's had enough to drink. She's grinning wide, giddy, and it has me matching her smile with my own. This girl is fucking incredible.

"There you are…come on let's get out of here. I've got cowboy's name, and I'm drunk. We need to go before I do something stupid." Mya's friend stammers on and yanks Mya by the arm away from me. Further away from me than I'd like especially now because we need to finish what I started.

I stand there dumbfounded with my eyes fixed on her until she's pulled out of view. I follow as a puppy would their owner, watching as they collect their coats, trying not to break my inquiry of her. She takes one last look for me over her shoulder before being pulled out of the tavern's front door. I'm dizzy with an overwhelming sense of exhilaration. I feel emotionally sated.

The DJ is on for the rest of the night. At the bar I sit with Dustin and revel in the lull as if I'm coming down off a high. Wyatt serves us a few beers as my brother, and I chat about the new ladies who breezed in tonight. It sounds like Dustin will need to break things off with his current flame since he met a new one tonight. He had a good laugh when I told him I had pulled Mya over earlier today.

The DJ plays for a few hours longer before I notice some of the regulars begin to head home. Shaking my brother's hand goodbye, I do the same. I go upstairs to my apartment, passing the supply closet door on the way. Mya's perfume still lingers in the air and it has me wishing we weren't interrupted.

I ready myself for bed, fall back into my pillows and close my eyes.

I imagine her. Her soft lips and full smile; her laugh now vivid in my memory. I recall her body tensing when I silenced her laugh with my kiss. I relive pulling up her dress and feeling the wetness on her underwear. My body starts to respond to my own recollection of Mya, and although that's where our encounter ended, I continue the reel in my mind. I imagine pulling her underwear aside and as I knew they would, my fingers slip inside effortlessly. With only that mental picture, I'm tipped over the edge. My cock stiffens, my hand takes over as I continue to imagine what the real thing might feel like.

6

Mya

Two hours ago

"*Oh my God, it was him. He was Officer Sex on Legs.*" I slur my words as Trisha, and I wait outside for our cab.

Wait. What?! Who!? She's puzzled. Several cabs pull up in front of Styne's Tavern. We picked one, and climbed in the back seat, falling all over each other giggling.

In my drunken state I had forgotten to tell Trisha about getting pulled over earlier that day. What I hadn't forgotten to tell her was the *why*.

On the ride home, I proceed to tell her the part of the story of being pulled over, fully elaborating on the details about how delicious the officer was. She apologizes profusely for removing me from the Tavern when I tell her he was *also* the super-hot guitar playing cowboy who she found me with.

"Oh my God, Mya, I don't think this could get any hotter. What was his name?" She asks.

"I don't know, I didn't get a chance to ask him," glaring fault at my drunk friend.

The cab pulls up to my house first. I give my friend a hug and tell the cab driver where his next location will be and pay for us both. I exit the cab stepping up and onto the sidewalk.

"Get some rest, you hussy. Call me in the morning!" Trisha screams to me out the window as the cab pulls away.

I turn to wave goodbye and the same vehicle I feared earlier today is now driving at a snail's pace past my house. I remain motionless until the car is out of sight. Even in my drunken state, my paranoia presents itself, reminding me that the drama I tried to get away from tonight, is still out there.

It's so late and I'm so tired. I grab the pile of unopened mail obviously thrown on my welcome mat. Inside I position my purse and keys in their usual places on the floor. I kick my boots off and tossed them aside too.

I'm not sure why but I tip toe to the kitchen to fetch myself a bottle of water. I look around timidly to be sure I am not being watched, and I strip off my clothes in the kitchen. I pull the hem of my dress up over my head and slip the night shirt on which I removed in this exact spot this morning.

Anyone I welcome into my house would consider me a slob. I leave evidence everywhere that I live here and live here comfortably. Tiptoeing again, I trace my steps back to my purse, knowing that's where my speeding ticket is. I find it buried and crinkled in the bottom of it under several shades of lipsticks and loose cash. I prance in bare feet to my bedroom, holding on tightly to my ticket, my mail, and my bottle of water.

I try to flatten out the ticket in search of a name. *The name which belongs to the cop, the cowboy, the Marine who stole my heart and robbed me of breath*— twice. I blink rapidly trying to clear my vision. I know I'm drunk but all I see on the ticket is a large note written in black marker.

Slow down beautiful and call me later if you're too scared to talk now. 555-2354. Cole.

There is no ticket!? I become dizzy; my thoughts start spiraling out of control. I'm in awe of the gentleman he is but pissed off that this whole time I never *actually* had a ticket. He knew that tonight. From our one-liners back and forth, he must have known I hadn't look at the ticket yet. Our encounter would have gone completely differently had I known I had his number.

"*Oh shit*," I mutter aloud.

He knows—or does he? He's a cop. Shit. The Olden's. Shit. I left the scene or did I. Fuck. Was I even at *a* scene, do I know something I shouldn't know? In frustration, I throw the ticket aside and collapse into my pillows. How the hell am I in this mess? I'm still feeling the effects of alcohol to sort this out now and my goddamn paranoia and adrenaline has my heart beating faster than normal.

I'm so tired. After a few minutes and a few deep breaths—thank you therapy— I settle down knowing that it's not a *real* ticket, which means no court, which means I never have to see Cole again. And if I never have to see him again that means no one knows I was at the Olden's that night.

I somehow convince myself, at least for tonight, that this will all blow over and that was my last fleeting thought before drifting off to sleep.

***

I wake the next morning with a headache, dry mouth and sick stomach. I'm nursing a hangover that rivals ones in college. I pull myself up and lazily gather myself together. I find the mail which I had thrown and scattered across my bed beside old magazines and an empty bag of pretzels from nights before. An unmarked envelope catches my eye. I remove the piece of paper and read the words typed on it.

WAS IT YOU?

I'm not sure if it was the cigarette smelling paper or my paranoia, but my stomach begins to turn. A volcanic eruption of nausea has me stumbling for the bathroom.

I am going to throw up.

***

By Sunday night I'm thinking less about creepy cars and the anonymous note and I am full on daydreaming about Cole, the cowboy. His strong hands touching me and the erotic words he whispered in my ear has left a euphoric pulse in my lady parts. Who am I kidding? Nothing can make that delicious pulse go away like the creepy note left on my porch, and worse the words that insinuate that this person knows about the Olden's.

I find the note which I tossed on the floor Friday night. I crumble it up and toss it in the trash. I decide to ignore it because it could mean anything. It doesn't have to be tied to the Olden's, or Pins or my past? Right? It's a question not a statement. He doesn't know. My paranoia is getting the better of me again and I decide to distance myself from all things Oldens, scary cars, gunshots, the police—Cole.

"Cole." I try his name on my lips as I reminisce about his finger tracing my lip and the sensation I got when he circled my folds through my underwear. What a fantastic night. I've never felt so desirable, so craved in all my life.

My heart only slightly wounded when I realize I'll never see him again. Since he didn't mention the Olden's Friday night, then he doesn't know nor need to know that I was there.

"I. Do. Not. want to get involved." I mumble sternly to myself.

It's safer, it's for the best if I just stay away; but I secure his ticket in the kitchen drawer anyway, just in case.

***

"It's $82.36. Ma'am, $82, thirty...?"

"Yes, sorry, I heard you." The cashier requests my attention as she's finishes ringing up my pencil skirt and top for tomorrow's meeting. Trisha and I have a huge opportunity and I need a fresh outfit to help seal the deal.

"Ma'am, $82.36—" she repeats again, her frustration obvious.

"Yes, yes, I'm sorry. It seems I've misplaced my credit card."

She huffs and throws her hands in the air as I exit the store leaving my outfit and her commission on the counter. I leave the store empty handed, wracking my brain about where my credit card could be.

"Fuck." I sulk, remembering exactly where it is.

***

Styne's Tavern looks even more charming during the day, looking more like enormous log cabin home than a bar. The air is crisp and cool, and the Autumn breeze gives me a chill. My nerves begin to bite as I take in my surroundings, it's deserted yet peaceful. Leaves fall freely from the trees and the loose one's crunch under my feet.

Except for one truck, the stony parking lot is empty. I have no idea who will be here, if anyone. I make my way up the steps to the vast porch which appears more decorative than it did the other night. The bar is dark, and the door is locked, but I knock anyway. I peek in through the window; the place is desolate. I make my way around the back part of the porch; another entrance appears propped open with a large planter housing a purple mum. It's inviting, so I do just that; I let myself in.

"Hello?" I call out to no one. The place is calm, very different than the other night. I make my way through the bar, peeking over the counter to see if I can spot my credit card. If I can just grab it and go, that would be the highlight of my day. But I don't find it. I reach the end of the bar, turn the corner and find myself in the hallway where Cole and I frantically ravished each other. Faint music emanates from around the corner, and a part of me excites with curiosity and hope that someone is here with my credit card. I follow where the music is coming from and find a set of stairs descending to the basement. *Shit.* If this isn't the beginning of a horror movie, I don't know what is.

"Hello?" I call out again cautiously, stepping heavily as I descend the stairs. My eyes adjust to the change in light as I take the final step onto the basement floor.

"Hello, I think I left my credit car—?"

My stomach begins to cartwheel as I look around the room, if you can call this a room. It's dim, but the light that is shining illuminates all the metal on display. A bed is positioned right in the middle of the room which has a red comforter spread neatly across the top. Ropes dangle from the bed posts and a choker rests where I imagine someone's head would be. The black leather contraptions hanging from the ceiling make me uncomfortable and though I'm shaking, my legs carry me to the glass cabinets which border the room.

As I get closer, I can see what the cabinets are filled with toys. Sex toys. Various size whips, and ropes, lots of hand cuffs, metal ones, furry and leather ones. Fuck me…what is this place? The second cabinet is lined with glass, rubber, and silicone dildos and plugs of all colors, shapes, and sizes. I briefly have time to examine the third cabinet when the music is turned off. I hear footsteps approaching, fuck. I stand frozen for fear of getting caught in the act but still mesmerized by my surroundings.

What the hell am I doing down here? Clearly whomever lives here, I've invaded their personal space, and I have no business being down here. I turn quickly, and I'm face to face with some, thing, a device. *Ouch, Fuck, I don't want to know what that is used for.*

The footsteps become louder, and I'm pulled back into the realism of this moment. I just found someone's dirty secret and I need to leave, now. I contemplate running back up the stairs but I'm too far away now. Plus, I wouldn't know what I'd do once I got up there, plus I need my credit card back.

Shards of fear slice through me when a man's silhouette stands firmly in the darkness. It's a fear I recognize, one all too familiar, and one I haven't felt in years. The fear of the unknown, of where I'll be struck, how long the bruise would last, and all the things I'll try to do so it won't happen again. My past is transpiring in front of my eyes as the silhouette stands like a statue. I begin to fear the worst; I found a room that I shouldn't have, and now I'm going to pay the price for trespassing.

The man steps into the light and all my defenses fail me when I see it's Cole. I calm immediately at the sight of him. Forgetting my displacement and I suddenly feel at ease and safe.

He looks as surprised to see me as I do him. Is this his place? What the fuck does he do down here? Fuck, that's what he does. Cop, cowboy, marine, and now masochist. The realization seems to last an eternity. I cycle quickly through the fear and wanting to vomit, to being safe and secure. It all has my head swirling and confused.

His shorts hang from his hips perfectly and his bare chest glistens with sweat. So much sweat I could bathe in it. His breathing is erratic like he just finished running. His arm falls to his side after wiping the sweat off his forehead, that's when I see it register. He sees me standing in his—*bar*?

With tentativeness, he takes a step in my direction, confusion spread across his face. He looks around the room and notices where we are. He raises both hands in defense as if to tell me "it's okay." As a precaution, I take a step backwards. He takes another one toward me, and I again, step back.

His eyes growing as wide as mine uncertain of my next move. I must be radiating fear. Am I scared? Should I be scared? If I am appearing scared of him, why don't I feel it? Why haven't I moved? I feel safe, right? I did just meet him; I know nothing about him. Well, I know enough now looking around this place.

Analyzing a man's body language is much of what I practiced thanks to my past, but I can no longer tell if it's the workout or rage that's causing his chest to rise and fall so heavily.

"Hi. er, I forgot my credit card—I think."

Our eyes lock, but he remains silent. I muster the strength to take another step backwards. My body vibrates from fear of his silence, or maybe the unknown of what he's going to do, I don't know which. Why doesn't he say something? I peek over my shoulder, another step or two and I'll be at the stairs. I'll leave and never come back. I'll get a new goddamn credit card.

But scared or not, this attraction between us is too much, it's exhilarating and exhausting all at the same time. The intensity from the other night is creeping its way back into my mind; my lower half clenching over all the fun to be had in this room.

Cole reaches in his back pocket with one of his surrendered hands and pulls out a card, my credit card. He gazes down at the card in his hand as he takes a few steps closer to me. My heart pumping faster, heating my core, with each step he takes.

"Mya Dylan."

My name on his lips sets me off. My inner muscles start pulsing and my fingers start vigorously tapping at my side. He just creepily said my name like I'm his next murder victim, yet I'm totally turned on.

"Yup. That's me. Look, I'm sorry. I let myself in. The door was open, and I heard the music, and—." I stammer along but stop instantly when he reaches me. I slowly lift and hold out my hand up suggesting he give me my card, but he ignores my speechless request.

"Mya. I was in the moment; I got carried away the other night. You left before I could tell you that." He insists.

He takes a last step into me, his eyes fixed on mine, our desire thick and palpable. He stands within inches of me. He knows I remember Friday night, and fear aside, my lady parts are still singing and are now dancing at all the possibilities in this room.

"Have you ever used any of this stuff?" I ask timidly, tilting my head up to look at him.

I surprise myself with my own question. My voice betraying all logical sense. Do I care to know? Why do I want to know? Just get your card Mya and leave, I lecture to myself. I am intrigued though, and this gorgeous man in front of me, shirtless, tan, muscular, could teach me a thing or two I'm sure. He smiles, oh my god he smiles. You know that fantasy that every girl has, the one where a strong man picks you up, cock still inside, and slams you against the wall. Yeah, well, that could happen right here, right now, but that's not me. Right? I've been slammed into enough walls.

Fuck. I turn and make a run for the stairs, but he grabs me by the wrist and pulls me to the back of the room. I begin to struggle viciously.

"Cole, I have to go." I cry. I can almost pull my arm a way, but he grips me tighter.

"Mya, stop, I'm not going to hurt you."

He aggressively pulls me around the corner to another area of the basement. It's a finished room much like the *bar* part. I don't even know what to call that room.

My voice struggles with each word, but somehow the words still roll on their own, begging him to let me go. He growls in frustration, returns my credit card to his back pocket, and restrains me in his arms. I'm the only one yammering, he hasn't said anything else, but our eyes are dancing back and forth in between my half ass attempts to free myself.

"Will you relax, you are not in there anymore. Stop struggling this is my gym, you're in my gym now." He pleads for my patience. Our heaving chests are saying enough, and once I do calm, I look around and take in my new surroundings. Gym equipment and lots of it.

He drops his arms and lifts me up in one sift motion. With his hands gripped tightly under my ass, he carries me to a table in the back of the room. My hands firmly grip around his shoulders, my fingernails clawing into his skin. It's erotic and terrifying all at the same time.

I want him, and he knows it. He knows I'm not truly afraid of him anymore. He sets my ass down on the table, pulls my knees up, and steps in-between them. He holds them along his hips continuing to analyze my reaction to him. He reaches in his pocket and retrieves my card, holds it up presenting it as proof, and places it next to me on the table. He stares into my eyes and begins breathing with me as if he's helping to regulate my breaths. His attempts are unsuccessful since I'm now panting under his touch. Breathless not in fear, but in pure lust and desire; I'm craving him, and he knows it.

"Leave it." He states, as a matter of fact, as he releases my leg. He slides his other hand from under my knee, down my calf and circles my ankle. He steps forward, pressing himself tight to my center. Our eyes lock, and in one rapid motion he pulls my ankle up, yanks my underwear aside and pushes a finger into my warmth. I gasp and cry out at the sudden onset of pressure. The desire and urgency he's exerting makes my whole body come alive. It's foreign, delivering sensations I've not felt before. He's craving me as he did that night at Styne's and I'm okay with that.

He pushes his finger in and out and before I'm ready for it, he inserts another, and then another. It's swift and erotic. My head involuntarily falls backward, absorbing every drop of pleasure he's giving me. He brings his lips to my chin, grazing it with kisses and sucking lightly on the tip. His own inhales deepen; he's enjoying himself. My acceptance to his assault is evident as my arousal echoes in the room. The air is thick, and the only sound other than my anticipated orgasm is his heavy breathing from bringing me to it.

His fingers are thick, and firm, and he knows I'm close. His pace slows, his fingers curl, and my inner muscles tighten around him.

I surrender, I let go completely and release onto him the fear, excitement, and paranoia that has been pent up for days. He brings my head to his chest as he slowly pumps his fingers and I reach my peak, spilling over every raw emotion I'm able to let go of. He remains quiet while my orgasm fills the room.

He's kept his word; he watched me come.

7

Cole

"Morning Pop. Did you bring me leftovers for lunch?"

I greet my father with a pound on the back before finding my seat in the briefing room.

"Morning, Cole," he cheers throwing me a bagged lunch from yesterday's dinner.

I made it to dinner at my folk's house but just barely. I sat in the gym for hours after Mya left. She left so suddenly. She left without giving me a chance to collect myself, or again explain my intent or what the fuck had just happened. What happened was I couldn't help it, I had to touch her, I had to feel her. I no sooner removed my fingers from her pussy, and she hopped off the table and ran out of the place. She was gone before I could comprehend her absence. She left and I still have no way to contact her, no legal way, anyway.

"Aw, a grown-ass man still has mama making his lunch," my brother mocks me but shuts up when Pop throws him his own bagged lunch. I also counter with my own quip about him going all soft for a pretty thing at Styne's Friday night.

"Yeah, whatever, man, I saw you too, all, oh baby" he mimics my hand and traces his own cheek. What he doesn't know is that gesture doesn't compare at all to her visit with me yesterday.

"Alright, quiet down, ladies, let's get started!" Captain barks settling the room. For the next thirty minutes all the officers including myself and Dustin listen intently to him as he outlines the days agenda. He ends the briefing always the same way. *"Be safe out there."* The room stirs, and the boys are on their feet. We all have our orders.

On my way out the door, Carol catches me mid step as I walk past the patrol office. Her hands are full as she struggles to carry a large box.

"Oh, Cole dear, the Dylan traffic stop. No ticket? Can I just trash it?" She questions trying to maintain her balance.

I take the bulky box from her hands offering her some relief. She sighs a thank you as I walk her to the adjacent office.

I love Carol, she's been with the department for thirty-seven years. I used to steal candy from her desk when I wandered around here as a boy. She always had spare toy guns waiting for me. She would keep the secrets I'd tell as I played detective.

"Yea trash it. I'm letting it go, it was her first ticket,"

I clarify for her as I set the box down on her desk and start for the door.

"Oh, Carol did the weekend bring anything new on the Olden case? I'm heading over there now."

She confirms with a nod and pushes her glasses up her nose, making the chains on the sides of her face rattle a bit. As she sifts through the pile of files on top her desk her glasses slowly drift down her nose. She pushes them up again, a ritual I've observed for years.

"Aha, here it is," she gleams handing me a file.

"Thanks, Carol." I kiss the top of her head as I would my grandmother. For all intents and purposes, she's like a grandmother to me. I walk out of the PD, down the steps to my truck.

"Ha-ha, bastards, I'm not on patrol," I sing secretly as I see Dave and Dustin head out in their cars.

***

I park outside the Olden's, looking around as if that one piece of the puzzle is going to jump out at me. I'm somewhat familiar with this couple, a few domestic disputes over the years. A son now grown and has moved away. A daughter local to the area but rarely visits. There's no evidence of grandkids or other close friends or family nearby. I blow on my coffee to cool it and I open the file that hopefully holds new information the patrolman brought in over the weekend.

A few neighbors have noticed a black jeep unfamiliar to the area, but nothing that raised suspicion for the deputies. The Olden's said someone was shooting near the house not *at* the house. But when asked, they can't think of anyone who would be that upset with them.

I read on. Two houses down, Ms. Brownell mentions a several joggers that night but it's all routine, it's a popular street for runners. There's nothing out of the ordinary here. Mr. Dickenson said he saw a shadow around a big tree in front of 56 S. Campbell Drive. That's right across the street. I look up from the file in search of the tree.

It sits curbside. Its thick trunk tells me the tree has seen more history in this town than any local. Its wide roots poke up from the ground causing the sidewalk to buckle and crack above them. Branches spray upward and outward over the street in a perfect dome with leaves that pop with Autumn colors. There's a nice collection of leaves at the base and this time of year, the leaves would crunch under your feet. If you're trying to hide, standing under this tree would not be the way to go.

Fuck. I curse as coffee spills in my crotch. I swipe it away while my eyes follow a welcome distraction out the front window. Mya Dylan.

Black yoga pants lined with pink stripes hug her curves and her pink top is snug to her chest. Her ponytail bangs from side to side as she runs. Her earbuds are in, she's focused, and she runs with discipline. I exit my truck and quickly make my way over to her before she passes. Not knowing exactly what I'm going to say, especially after yesterday, but she stops running instantly when she sees me.

"*Hi.*" I'm an idiot; my spontaneous greeting betrays me.

"Hi," she responds beaming. She removes her earbuds and bends forward. Her hands rest on her knees as she tries to catch her breath.

"Out for a run?" Oh fuck. I've just mentally punched myself in the forehead and will need to move on quickly before I out-do my idiot status and venture into pure stupidity.

Her grin widens and she bows her head blushing. With her chest still heaving, her breasts hurdle themselves at me with every breath as if they are tempting me to come closer.

"Yesterday was—" I start to explain the very best I can what transpired yesterday, but she pauses and then looks up at me.

"I got your 'ticket' by the way. Thank you." Her voice now timid, soft, and delicate as she tries to change the subject. She's saying so much more than that simple thank you, but I can tell she's not ready to talk about yesterday.

"Well, you have my number now if you ever need anything." I take a step closer to her, responding to the same lure that pulls me in every other time.

"Is that the cop's number or the cowboy's number?" She teases, showing me the smile that had me wild at Styne's Friday night.

"Baby, I'll be whoever you want me to be, whenever you want me to be it." We catch each other's eyes playfully and I take yet another step forward as the intensity builds.

"Why do you call me baby?" She titters while pulling her eyes away to take in her surroundings. I recall her doing the same thing during the traffic stop.

"I call everyone baby, baby. It's a cowboy thing."

Still smiling, she replaces her earbuds and begins walking away and just when I start to feel that familiar emptiness, she turns to face me. Jogging backwards now, she blows me a kiss, mouths the word goodbye, and holds her hand flat to her chest as if she is holding her heart.

In that moment, feeling like a boy at an amusement park, I realize that Mya Dylan is someone I need in my life.

Watching Mya now, I recall how Paige's infidelity broke me. I had never felt pain and emptiness like I did when I found Paige in bed with someone else, or the suffocating loneliness that followed. But for the first time since, I stand in the middle of the street, watching a woman who has completely taken me by surprise. She literally sped into my life and has made me forget everything that came before her. She might be running away from me now, but she put a heartbeat back in my chest that wants for nothing but time with her. I'm breathing again.

My pocket starts vibrating, breaking me from my revelation. *"It's Cole,"* I answer, my eyes still glued on Mya's ass as she rounds the corner.

"What did you say? The caller has my attention. *"I'm standing right next to that damn tree."*

"I'm on my way back. Keep him there"

***

Back at the station, I'm received by an exasperated and overly eager Captain. *"We have a witness, Cole. This could be the break we need."*

My pace exceeds his and has him scurrying to keep up. He's struggling between his hurried breaths informing me that the Olden's neighbor Bill is here in room #4 being questioned. It's obvious my father is itching to get to the bottom of this case before it runs cold. I walk into the interrogation room just as Dave is drilling a man about his relationship with Mrs. Olden.

"I told you, it is one time twenty years ago. She's religious, she said she'd never divorce him, so it was over as quickly as it had started."

"You don't say." I'm callous as I rudely interject myself into their conversation, but it didn't seem to faze him. The man continues.

"I'm only here now because Brad and Angel are in trouble and I can help. God help me, she'll be pissed but I can help. Call it...trying to right my wrongs."

"Who is this?" I'm pace the room annoyingly as I play catch up.

Dave stands in front of me to hide his explanation of Bill. *"This is Bill, he lives across the street from the Olden's...the "quiet neighbor."* I look over Dave's shoulder trying to sift through my mental filing cabinet. I now recognize him as the man in his mid-sixties who peeps in on the action across the street at the Olden's but never has anything to offer the police— until now?

"Why now, why are you here?" I shoot straight to the point.

"I heard the yelling and gunshots. I looked outside, you know, through my window to see what the commotion was. I saw Angel on the ground and Brad standing over her. His hands were flying around, pressing into his temples as if to release a headache." Bill pauses, grasping and fumbling with the cigarette in hand. *"I looked out the window again and someone caught my eye. A woman. She was standing next to the maple tree in my front yard. She ducked and*

disappeared as quickly as I spotted her. It all happened so fast."

"*That's it. That's all you saw. A woman standing next to your tree.*" I'm completely frustrated with the lack of details Bill is *not* offering about the mystery woman or the shooter. I throw a couple of mug binders on the table and I leave, allowing Dave to take over the questioning. I head for the Captain's office as I hear Dave confirm with Bill that he heard two distinct gunshots.

"*I've read the reports. Pop. There is no mention of anyone else seeing what happened that night, but someone was there and accidentally or purposefully they shot Angel. Did the weekend team interview everyone on the street?*"

"*Yes, Cole, everyone on the South end of Campbell Road.*"

We both sit in silence, pondering the case and trying to come up with our next play. My father broke the silence first.

"*Your mother wants to know who made you all smiles at dinner last night. And it best not be Paige.*" I peer at him out of the corner of my eye and smirk at my father knowing he must deliver his wife's message.

His hands raise in surrender *"Your mothers' question son. Hers, not mine."*

"It's no one, just someone I met at Styne's." I say chuckling as I push myself up from the chair.

"See ya, Pop." I grin purposely giving him nothing, knowing he must face my mother's interrogation later. He struggles to stand and chases me out of the office.

"A name, son.... she'll want a name!" He shouts down the hallway at me. I motion goodbye to him, waving my hand over my head. I need to finish up a few things before I head back out and inspect myself a goddamn maple tree.

***

"LSPD *Cole Styne*" I answer the desk phone.

"Colton."

A woman's voice. I recognize it immediately. She's the only one who calls me Colton, other than my parents but even they have become used to calling me Cole. Her soft voice ricochets in my ear and a continuous loop of memories come reeling in. My name on her lips sends shock waves to my heart, which sting and pinch much like it did the night I found her. My heart is beating fast, my hands become sweaty, and my nerves are now rattled.

I sit upright at my desk and scribble her name down with an exclamation mark. I look around the PD for

68

Dustin and snap my fingers requiring his attention when I spot him. I hold up the piece of paper showing him her name. His jaw drops. He frantically finds a pen and paper and writes back, shrugging his shoulders in question as he does. MYA?? It reads. I return his shrug and drop my head to bring my focus back to the woman on the other end of the phone.

"Paige. It's been months." Although I want to reach through the phone and touch her skin to be sure it's her, her name comes out more fractious than a sigh of relief.

"Colton," she whispers. I can hear her voice breaking, she's crying.

"It's Cole, Paige," I correct her without acknowledging her tears. Colton died the day I realized her betrayal. I loved her wholeheartedly, but she betrayed me and for me it ended that day. Her nervous tone is speaking volumes about what she wants to talk about. My gut tells me to hang up, but I don't, and I wait for her to speak again.

"I miss you. Can I see you?"

I chuckle to myself remembering I used a similar line on Mya, but it's not what Paige means at all.

I visualize mine and Mya's intimate encounter at Styne's and again in my gym. I slide my fingers across my chin to steady my head, inhaling deeply wishing I could still smell her on them. My fingers start tapping furiously on the desk as I remember how her pussy tightened around them. My daydream is interrupted, killing my pulsing hard-on when Paige forces my name through the phone.

I inhale sharply, sit back deep into the chair looking around the department for a distraction. I run my hand through my hair exhaling again trying to sort out in my mind what she just said. I don't have anything to say to her. Anything I did want to say, I didn't, and I said it to the wall. I have no unfinished business with her, but curiosity is getting the better of me.

"I'm free Thursday for lunch. Thirty minutes, it's all I have, Paige. I'm working on a case."

She sounds pleased and that's annoying as fuck. We confirm the time and place just as Dustin approaches my desk and I toss the phone into its cradle.

"What are you doing, Brother?"

He's somewhat impressed that I have two beautiful women seeking my attention, but annoyed that I'm giving Paige the time of day. I remind him that it's only lunch, that I have only just met Mya and not to worry about it.

He turns on his heels making a smartass comment about making *the bitch* pay for lunch. I return to the stack of warrants on my desk and peek at the computer screen for the time. I begin fidgeting with the pen, tapping it repeatedly and rapidly on the files. After probably 30 seconds, I look to my cell phone for the time. Time has slowed down, I'm preoccupied.

Paige is back.

8

Mya

I am up early Thursday morning. Trisha and I have our client meeting later this evening, one of many that were rescheduled. She and I have prepped for weeks for this meeting and we are certain it's a done deal. Dinner tonight, we hope, is just a formality.

Until then though, I have somewhere I need to be.

I throw my oversized pants and t-shirt on, pull my hair up into a high ponytail, and prepare for the drive out to Somerset.

Soon, I make the right-hand turn just before the bend, the one at the yellow "Hidden Drive" road sign. It leads to a long gravel road then to a large property secured by a metal gate. The gate is hugged by white stone columns topped with colorful mums.

Past the gate and down the driveway, which is lined with full vibrant maple trees, a stone cottage sits in the middle of a clearing. It's a hidden gem, something straight out of a fairytale with rolling mountains off in the distance.

It was a retirement home my parents built after my brother and I graduated from high school. It's the home they planned to grow old in. Fate had other plans for my father, but my mother has remained here alone with her flower and vegetable gardens to fuss over.

"Hi, mom." I finally have my arms around her, she's my best friend. I hold on to her tight and I release the breath I know I've been holding onto for days.

"Hi, Sweetie. Are you okay? You seem shaken." I nod but there's no fooling her.

"This isn't still about Evan, is it Mya? There's other fish in the sea."

I roll my eyes. *"Mom, no, and you know I hate that saying."*

She wraps my arm around hers and we walk together to the cottage, still insisting there's something bothering with me.

We spend the early morning on her back porch sipping hot tea and chatting. I tell her about my last few days and how I met Cole in the most unusual way. I fill her in on the speeding ticket, Styne's Tavern, and all things heart pumping. As expected, the part of my story involving the ticket has the "mom" look coming out. The one where the glasses fall to the tip of her nose and she looks over the top of them, tilting her head and pointing her finger like I'm in big trouble. My younger brother rarely saw the look. He was the perfect child and in my parent's eyes, did no wrong. I on the other hand, saw the look frequently, so frequently I could uncannily mimic it. I was rowdy. I got myself into a lot of trouble, which probably has caused my mom some of her gray hair.

I struggle to stand as my legs have become weak from rocking. She puts an arm around my shoulder, obviously sensing I've already beat myself up over the ticket. She doesn't ask any more questions, which I'm thankful for. She doesn't need to know why I was speeding. I left that part out. We'll save that for another day.

In the garage, we chat on and off about my dad as she shows me her latest autumn floral arrangements. Other than her tiny corner, the garage is exactly how my dad left it.

On our way out, we pick up wicker baskets and wander through her gardens. We fill the baskets with sticks, pebbles, and pinecones which she'll later use for one of her crafty ideas. Then, over the next few hours, I help her clean the cottage and prepare meals for the weekend.

Without my father around my mother won't pay for handyman, so I secretly keep a honey-to-do list which my brother and I will chip away at when we're here visiting. I finish washing the breakfast dishes and put them away while she is changing her clothes. She's getting ready for late afternoon tea with Alice down the road.

My mother returns fully dressed in her floral top, khaki pants, and dark tan flats. She's pinned her hair up on the sides and put a little blush on her cheeks. She looks cute. I love that she still fusses over herself even without someone here to notice. I kiss her goodbye and tell her I'll be back soon.

9

Cole

I pull up outside Styne's and as if she still belongs here, I see her car parked in her old spot. I've spent the last three days trying to make sense of her phone call and there is her car, sitting there as if she never left.

The Tavern won't open until later, so it's quiet, peaceful, and snow is making its first appearance. I shut the truck off and sit quietly for a few moments. I stare out the side window, looking at the vast cabin and the beautiful scene behind it.

It's cold and I can see my breath now that I've sat idle for a few minutes. I rub my hands together and blow in them trying to release the sting from the cold. I tear myself from the seat of my truck and step out into the dusting of snow, leaving traces of where I've been, and where I'm going.

I walk casually, hearing the knock of my boots on the wooden steps as I ascend to the deck.

I recall the last time I saw Paige at Styne's, in our apartment upstairs. How she ripped my entire future away from me in a matter of fifteen seconds. She's to blame, yes, but there was once a time she could do no wrong. I loved her unconditionally, I saw only her and now she's just behind this door, waiting for me.

My hand begins shaking as the nerves have started to bite. *"Jesus."* I pull myself together. As I grip the door handle, I convince myself that when I walk in there and see her, I won't feel that way again. I won't feel the way I felt when I was in love with her. When time stood still, and the only way forward was with her.

Immediately, as soon as I cross the saloon doors, I feel the thickness in the air. It's becoming harder to swallow, to catch my rattled breath, even harder still as I walk further into the Tavern. I start up the stairs to my apartment but my steps falter when I see her in my peripheral. I turn and spot her sitting alone in the middle of the dining room and as if there is a beacon surrounding her, I'm off the step and walking toward her aimlessly.

Her blonde hair is shorter but her tiny stature is all I remember it being. I could lift her up with such ease. For the first time in months I don't have to wonder what it'd be like to see her again. She's here, but there's no desire to run to her, to hug or touch her; I'm just unmoved. She is a wonderful sight though and I'm in awe that she's back. But why?

I maintain my composure giving nothing away. I walk over to the bar and pour myself a drink. I nod to her in question, but she shakes her head declining the offer. The room is silent with only my boots and clanging of glass echoing in the vast space. I tread lightly to where she is, pulling out a chair opposite her and sitting down. I casually cross my ankle atop my opposite knee, and I wait. After exactly two uncomfortable minutes of silence and our eyes fixed on one another she grins and begins to speak.

"Do you remember when Wyatt used to drink over there with Russ and one night, he became too drunk to serve?"

I just about spit out my drink as we break into a roar of laughter. I do remember.

Wyatt my grey haired, extremely fit 72-year-old raw cowboy bartender. His wife Marjorie passed away right after he retired and since then he's become the biggest flirt in this town. He's always been ready for a good time and the women, young and old, fall to his charms. He was the cook at the BBQ joint that was here prior. I bought the place and made it into Styne's. He loved it here as much as I did so I kept him on, and like any old western cowboy it was normal for him to drink with the regulars.

"That's the last time I allowed him to drink on the job," I add to her story.

"Right, right, and wasn't that the first and only time Styne's had a karaoke night?" She pushes through her laughter. It's a beautiful laugh and with the tension now broken I'm the one to speak next.

"You and I did have some good times here P—" She doesn't let me finish.

"Oh, Colton."

I don't correct her this time.

"I really messed up and I'm so sorry for hurting you."

I just stare at her in disbelief. Watching her lips as she continues to talk and apologize for all her wrongdoings. How she should have been stronger and should have waited for me to come home from Iraq. She continues to say she ruined a good thing and we could be happy right now if she hadn't messed things up. *"It's over with him,"* she states, *"has been for months,"* she adds.

She continues describing in detail, memory after memory that we shared. When we met, parties we went to, what she felt like the first time we made love. My proposal and how embarrassed she is in front of the stadium, so on and so on. My eyes glaze over listening to my life being replayed for me. The frailty in her voice has my heart pinching with empathy. I watch as her tears fall one by one, making no attempt to wipe them away. Are those tears for my benefit? So, I can see how much pain she is in? So, I can understand that she's speaking the truth.

My hand grips tightly around my whiskey glass, I haven't moved nor, have I spoken. I just sit there for several minutes listening to her. I see her lips moving, I hear her words but I'm not listening anymore. I'm emotionless. She leans over the table and grazes my hand with her fingertips. I let her. She's testing my reaction to her, to see if I'll recoil, if I'm angry with her still. She has my eyes and I can't pull them away now. With a rerun of our life together being laid out for me, I am paralyzed.

She stands and grabs my hand, pulling me up from my chair. Her hand is small in mine; I have no sense of how tightly I'm holding it. She pulls me to the back stairwell which leads to my apartment. I let her. Her perfume leaves a trail for me to follow and I do, as if I'm in a trance, mindlessly following a siren to my death.

She closes the apartment door behind her, turns to me, and takes a step into my body. My hands are at my side. My large frame swallows her tiny one, just like it used to. I refuse to touch her, but my breathing becomes erratic, which suggests that I am okay with her proximity. I know I should speak up and stop this derailing train we're on, but I can't. I can't stop the inevitable. I am under her spell.

It's silent, the room is airless. Her eyes look up into mine as she unzips my pants. She reachs her hand down between my skin and boxers and wraps her hand around my growing shaft. With the past now present and in the forefront of my mind, my cock has a mind of its own.

"Are you seeing anyone?" She murmurs against my tightly closed lips. She starts to grasp and pull harder on my dick causing it to expand in her hand. I already start to feel the pangs of guilt tugging as Mya immediately flashs to my mind, but I don't speak up.

"I didn't think so." She boasts—she's so full of herself, a vain bitch, yet here I am about ready to fuck her.

She lifts herself onto her toes and presses her lips into mine. I want to push her away, I do, but my body goes into autopilot, functioning in the way it did before, when we were together, in love, and happy. My hands grip under her ass and I lift her up. Her legs find their own way over my waist. Our lips slowly lock together as I hesitantly submit and soon our tongues engage.

I take her to the couch knowing that because of her, the bedroom is off limits. I fuck Paige with the same technique I always used on her. Her moans sound the same, her hands trace my body the same way, and even her orgasm hasn't changed. When we finally reach our climax, I feel vacant.

I fall back onto the couch speechless and unsated. When her release has ended, she falls on top of me resting her head on my chest. I lay there on my back with my hands resting above my forehead. Even with the weight of her naked body on top of me, I completely regret what just happened. I keep my hands secured trying not to touch her any more than I must.

***

Later that day, I update my father on today's happenings leaving out the part about my extended lunch break.

"I need you back in the field again tomorrow. Retirement is teasing me son— its's-a-knocking." I grin at his statement, pull him in for a tight father-son hug and a pound on the back.

My father's tone is tinted with trepidation. The gray-haired man has put many years in at the PD. He and mom are now ready to retire to Florida. However, there are a handful of cases he feels he needs to wrap up before that move can take place.

I imagine the Olden case has the first gun shots heard in Lorry Springs in twenty years. The last major incident in this town was about ten years ago. A drunk driver caused a major pile up on Route 10 and the driver was never found. He or she used an alias, was able to dump the rental car and we never found the person who caused it. A lot of people were injured, and a few lost their lives. My father cannot go into retirement with another cold case tied to his tenure.

"I'll bring the file home tonight and look it over again. Tell Mom not to worry and I'll see you guys soon for dinner."

***

Through my front door, I juggle files in one arm and take-out burgers in the other. It's not thirty seconds before I realize I'm alone. I haven't heard from Paige the rest of the day after our moment of "familiarity." She's gone again. There's no note, no evidence that we were even here this afternoon. She just vanished. It's as if I just awoke up from a dream and today didn't happen at all. Paige walked back into my life and as quickly as I made her come, she's back out of it. I am done.

The deafening silence is back. *"I need a fucking dog."*

Dropping the contents of my hands angrily on the kitchen countertop, I ponder how a dog wags its tail and is happy to see you after you've been gone all day. It barks and its claws tap on the tile which would be music to my fucking ears.

In the hallway, I drag my fingers across the broken sheetrock telling myself the same lie, I do every time— I'll fix it this weekend. I secure my firearm, remove my badge, and hang my uniform neatly in the closet.

After my shower, I turn the game on that I DVR'd from last Monday. My attempt to fill the silence with something other than my own movements. I collect myself a few beers, grab the brown bag with my burger and plop on the green suede couch that I fucked Paige on earlier. My ass sinks deep down into the cushions. I do love this couch, it's a hand-me-down but I'm comfortable as hell with my legs extended and my feet crossed on the coffee table in front of me. My spare beer sits just behind me on the couch table where I have the last three months of hunting magazines and newspaper clippings. I take a bite of my burger, lay the Olden file across my lap, and start flipping through it.

There is nothing unusual about this call other than the unknown shooter near the house. Okay, that's a big fucking deal, but Brad said he didn't see who did it. It was late and dark, so the likelihood of neighbors, other than Bill, offering anything substantial is low.

The Olden's have two adult children whom they report that they haven't seen in years. Their son is a real winner from the sounds of it. He did a nickel for sexual assault and battery when he was 22. Their daughter lives alone uptown with her fiancé.

Who'd they piss off? Why a drive by, and if it wasn't them the shooter was shooting at, then who? I spit the questions out rapidly as if I am interrogating someone else in the room, yet no one is here. The story hasn't wavered, and I still come up empty. I continue reading the report but nothing noteworthy is standing out. I decide my next step is to investigate and seek out people living on North and South Campbell Road, investigate the Olden's son, their other neighbors, anyone, someone must know something more.

My eyes are heavy. I pitch my head back to check the time. It's 11:50 pm, right on time. Late at night is the hardest for me. It's the stillest and quietest moments of my day. It's when Paige's absence and betrayal are felt the deepest. It's when pops of gunfire ricochet in my ears triggering my PTSD.

I sit for only a minute longer before my thoughts turn on me and I hear the vivid screams of Rhett. I toss the Olden file aside and rub the burn out of my eyes. I immediately see Paige grinding steadily and hearing the growls of that asshole. Feelings of guilt and disgust rip through me as I recall my own mistake with her today. Fucking her today was routine. I fucked up. I knew it as it was happening. I push the thoughts of her away only to have them replaced with echoes of bullets and Rhett screaming for me to run. The two memories are on constant replay.

"Fuck," I stammer...

I get up steadying my feet on the carpet and make my way to the bedroom. As if they call out to me, I slide my fingers across the holes in the wall, dipping my fingers in and scrapping the tips across the broken sheetrock. Again, muttering to myself the already broken promise. I know damn well those holes will be there for a while longer. I make it to the bed, collapse, and for a moment consider jerking off. I excite myself over the release I might get from it, but instead I close my eyes and pass out.

10

Mya

"Trisha, loosen your knickers, sister, and calm down. I'll be there soon." I roll my eyes into the phone. *"I'm not going to get to work any faster if you don't let me hang up."* I end the call abruptly and toss my cell phone on the bed.

Trisha and I have worked for the same accounting firm for the past two years. We are busy as the holiday season is approaching. People get crazy with all the money they want or feel they must spend. Suddenly accountants are their friend because somehow, we make the money appear from nowhere.

This morning however, Trisha and I have a wrap up meeting with Missouri Holdings and she's hot over the fact that I'm running late. This contract could boost our career, making us partners at the firm. Dinner with them went extremely well and they called an early meeting for this morning.

I zip up my black pencil skirt, squeeze my toes into 5-inch stiletto heels with ankle straps and tuck a silver rope necklace into the "V" of my top. I'm fumbling over my second earring and looking for my handbag when the doorbell rings. I grab my phone, handbag and hustle to the door as it rings again. I answer the door. My breath hitches slightly as liquid warmth collects in my lady parts.

"It's you."

"It's me."

He stands there with his full lips slightly parted and appears as dazed and shocked as I imagine I look. It's been a little while since I've seen Cole Styne, the cop, the cowboy, the marine. He's wearing a navy suit with his badge proudly on display around his neck. He looks official and cop-like but he's glaring at me as if he just cracked a case wide open.

"Cole, hey—what are you doing here?" I ask nervously.

"I'm actually here for work." He doesn't hesitate, and he continues talking trying to hide a smile. *"When I pulled you over—you look fucking beautiful by the way—I, um, noticed you lived on this road."* I blush. His comment about my appearance makes me swoon and puddle all over the floor like a high school girl with a crush. His blue eyes and the sharpness of his jawline is distracting at hell. His eyes are wide, and he seems to be distracted by my appearance; he continues speaking as he runs his fingers through his hair.

"There was an incident not long ago on the south end of your road and I'm following a few leads today. Do you know anything about it?" He pauses waiting for me to reply.

"Um, I don't know. What happened?" I'm trying to stay focused, but if he's a good cop at all, he'll know that I already know what happened. It's been all over the news.

"Nothing you should worry about, but you still have my number, yes?"

I nod wordlessly.

"I suppose it's my lucky day then." He releases his breath, he's flirting. I hear his voice, but I am no longer listening. My head becomes fuzzy as I recognize the nauseas feeling in the pit of my stomach. A black jeep sits idle, just a house or two down, across the street.

Stalking there like a black panther stalks a rabbit. I can barely make out a face but there is one there staring at me out the front window. All the blood drains from my face as my paranoia disorients me, like a drug. I become dizzy and weak, I can't focus my thoughts or my vision. I begin to tremble uncontrollably, and I steadily bring my eyes back to Cole.

"*Mya?*" His hand grips my shoulder as he offers a comforting squeeze.

"*Mya.*" He tries again to collect me, but his efforts are useless. My eyes are back on that jeep.

"*Mya, baby…*" He presses firmly through his teeth, but I still don't respond, and he's had enough. He grabs my shoulder, pushes himself past me and pulls on my hand for me to follow. He pushes the door closed behind him. Just as the door slams shut, the jeep speeds away making the departure obvious. Cole turns toward the squealing tires, but he sees nothing.

He pins me against the wall, his front presses into mine trying to immobilize my trembling. I'm restrained, but my body continues to shake involuntarily. Before I'm finally able to draw my attention back to him I look around to be sure we are alone inside my house.

"*Cole, I'm in a hurry, I have to go,*" and on cue my phone starts ringing in my hand.

"See?" I hold the phone up in protest hoping I won the attempt to leave.

"Put it on speaker," he orders. His voice is deep, controlled, and dominant, an all too familiar tone, so I obey.

"Trisha." My eyes drill into his as I display my annoyance with his outrageous demand.

"Listen, I don't know what's keeping you. Missouri Holdings said they can do one o'clock instead if that's good for you. Lucky for us, they had a key decision maker running late as well. Just get your ass in here ASAP." The line disconnects. Under his unwavering scrutiny, Cole seizes the cell phone from my trembling hand.

"Sounds like your morning just freed up." His jaw is tight, and his eyes are rigid but at the same time full of worry. His large hands are now holding my waist trying to keep me still. Something about Cole is different. He has the same dominance that I'm used to, but I don't fear him. He makes me feel safe. His hands are firm, but I know they won't hit me, they'll comfort me.

"Jesus, Mya. You're still shaking." He sounds genuine.

"Cole, you are here on police business, right? Ask me what you came here to ask me. Otherwise, I need to go."

"Mya, you're not going anywhere until you tell me what is going on." He's hard-pressed for an answer to a question he hasn't asked yet. He is demanding details from me; details I don't have, or at least I don't know I have.

"Is this the cop or the cowboy asking me?" I argue through my pressed lips, catching him off guard. I can't do this with him right now and he knows it. He releases me. I slide out from under the weight of his body. In a brief last attempt, he tries to catch my wrist, but I slip past him running out the front door. I quickly get in my car realizing only when I am well down the road that I've left him alone in my house.

***

It's 12:50 in the afternoon and though my nerves haven't settled from this morning, I'm ready and prepared to sell the firm to Missouri Holdings, which I could possibly do in my sleep.

Missouri Holdings is a tech company out of California which invests in first time business owners and entrepreneurs. Since taking on European partners, they are looking for a new accounting firm. This is a career making fourteen-million-dollar contract which will set Trisha and I up for partnerships at the firm. Therefore, for the next three hours, I catapult Cole and the black jeep out of my mind and do what I do best.

"Success, Bitches!!!!" Trisha screams across the office just as the elevator door closes with the Missouri Holdings management team aboard. The whole place goes wild.

"You two nailed it," one says. *"Congratulations"* someone shouts, and more and more cheers come from the sidelines. I give my lifelong friend and partner a hug and make our way through the masses of colleagues. The last few hours were fantastic. I was in my zone, talking business and numbers, forgetting all about the latest drama in my life.

"Oh my God, we must celebrate Friday night. Styne's?" Trisha invites questioningly as we settle into my office.

"I want to see Dustin again. We've only had coffee a few times since we met. I'm going crazy not seeing him. I glare at her stunned that she's becoming so attached to a man, any man.

"I thought cowboys were supposed to be speedy and smooth about asking us out on dates and shit." She continues loudly as she leaves my office. I roll my eyes at her dramatic exit as she throws high-fives and absorbs more compliments from our peers.

With the success of our meeting behind us, Trisha and I take the rest of the day off. I dread going home possibly to the cop I left there this morning. But I'm secretly eager to go back to Styne's to see my cowboy. I wonder if seeing each other again will result in the same exhaustive manhandling he's so expert in, maybe even more so after our tiff this morning.

***

I arrive home to find it minus one cop car, for which I'm thankful but nonetheless a bit disappointed. I crave his attention. The desire for me he exudes makes me come alive. Even though he appeared raging mad this morning, the powerful embrace he surrounded me with was reassuring.

I shiver. The cool autumn air screams that winter is just around the corner. I take in my surroundings before I get out of my car to be sure it is safe. I swiftly take my front steps, my heels slipping on the dusting of snow that has been falling lightly since this morning.

My eyes drop to a plain white envelope sitting boldly on the welcome mat. My stomach curls sending bile into my throat.

"Shit."

I pick up the letter and look behind me to see if anyone is nearby. No one. I slip through my front door, closing it tightly and locking it behind me. I kick off my heels and begin pacing the living room floor, dropping my keys on one pass, my bag on another, and then whatever

94

other contents are in my hands, until the only thing left is the envelope.

I can't look at it yet. I must wait until I am mentally equipped to handle whatever it says. My legs carry me to the kitchen. I gingerly place the envelope on the table. I nervously pour a glass of wine, take a breath, and finally sit down in front of the envelope. I inhale deeply, close my eyes and pull out the note. As soon as I'm brave enough to open my eyes, I read.

You whore. Getting chatty with the cops? I wouldn't say too much or my next shot won't hit her; it'll hit you.

***

I begin to tremble. I know I'm alone in the house but suddenly I feel like I'm being watched. There's a presence in my vicinity which runs my blood cold. It is real now. My paranoia has something tangible to latch on to. As much as I didn't want to be a part of that night, I was, I am.

I sit for hours with the lights on. Quiet. Disoriented and scared. The only sound is the hypnotizing tick of the kitchen clock and the hum of the refrigerator.

Tick. Tick. Tick.

I'm not sure how much time has passed before I'm flooded with possible solutions. I could call Trisha or my mom, but won't that put them in danger? I can't do that to them. I should just go to the police, but then he'll shoot me. Or maybe I can just tell Cole, his protective nature and his "ticket" must mean he'll know what to do. But Cole *is* the police, *shit*. I consider it a minute more, contemplating the risks, when a knock at the door startles me. I am immediately vigilant as if *he* had just heard my plan to tell the police. Another knock causes me to jump and the closer I get to the door; I can hear him. I recognize the voice.

"*Cole*," I whisper nervously knowing he shouldn't be here. Him being here is putting his life at risk, my life at risk.

I barely have the door open before he forces his way through. He takes me by the waist locking his eyes with mine as he kicks the door closed behind him. His hands wrap cleanly around my small figure. He stalks his way through my house taking me with him in his grasp as if he knows where he is going. His presence is commanding. His movements are fast and disciplined. I'm lifted off my feet; he's being gentle with me. My butt is rested down on the countertop. He tries to steady me again as his hands find their way from my hips to my shoulders. My breathing is erratic, and my body trembles with anticipation of the unknown. His hands come up to the nape of my neck and he wraps his fingers cleanly around my throat. He squeezes lightly, making the fear I feel real. My eyes grow wider the longer I stare at him. His pressure increases and I start to feel the pressure behind my temples. I'm scared, and he wants me to feel scared, but I don't fear him, I'm intrigued. He's not trying to hurt me; the pressure is just enough for me to take notice. He's trying to distract me; he wants me to forget what is scaring me and to focus on him alone.

Then, one of his hands falls to my back and the other to the back of my head. He pulls me into his broad muscular chest and holds me silently. I fall apart and begin to sob. He hushes me for several minutes, caressing my hair, like a parent would comfort a small child.

"Mya look at me," the low grumble of his voice is reassuring.

He tries to lift my chin to bring my face to his, but I pull away.

"Look at me, dammit. This is me, baby, just me, the cowboy, not the cop. Help me understand why every time I see you; you're shaking and frightened." His tone is hard and pressing for an answer.

His thumbs tug at my bottom lip as he wipes my tears away. I surrender my stubbornness and give him my eyes, pleading with him to distract me from the hell I've found myself in. He pulls my hair away from my sticky tear-soaked face and holds my head between his hands. I feel my body settle and soon the trembling subsides.

Something about his touch calms me, warms me to my core, and I feel safe.

Cole is safe.

The room grows quiet as my sobs are now only a whimper. I watch as his lips part, his tell, he's secretly craving me. His eyes dart swiftly around my face, analyzing it, to see if the fear is gone, and if the desire he's feeling is reciprocated.

My face is held in the only position it can be between his firm hands. The intensity is building, and it has us both confused, not knowing what to do with these sparks firing between us. But then, with one step forward he swoops in taking my mouth hard. His craving evident and saturated with lust. His tongue licks and tugs at my bottom lip until I allow him entry. When I do, he pushes even harder into the kiss, so hard I can taste the salt of my own tears. I want more. I lift my hands to his shoulders, and he flinches slightly. I don't know if I hurt him, but I quickly reposition to the back of his neck holding him in place. My tongue joining his, twisting together in a sweet slippery battle.

I release a timid moan into his mouth, and he rips himself free, leaving me with my lust exposed and dripping on the countertop.

I sit stunned, my hands positioned in the air as if he is still in them. Why is he stopping this? I find myself sitting humiliated after his dramatic change in demeanor. Neither one of us say anything. I lower my arms slowly and watch as he walks away. His back muscles ripple as he moves, they're so pronounced I can see them through his shirt. He rubs his left shoulder as if to rub a pain away. His hands fly through his hair, pulling and tugging at it like he is being tortured, like he has just done something horribly wrong and he's ridden with guilt. He freezes at the kitchen table. Something caught his attention and it hits me too. I know what he's spotted. My stomach sinks and I fear what his response will be. I look over at almost the same moment he turns back to me and roars.

"You're fucking lying to me!"

11

Cole

"*You're being threatened?*" My voice booms through her house.

"*Cole, no, you don't know what you're talking about.*"

"*Tell me I'm wrong, Mya.*" I proceed to read from the note. I won't call her a whore, so I skip that part. I stuff the note into my pocket. My way in the moment of protecting her.

"What night, Mya, the Olden shooting? Were you there? Are you the woman behind the tree?"

I see her eyes glaze over and that's all the confirmation I need.

"I thought you came here as the cowboy?" she counters, trying to change the subject. I walk over to her. She quickly hops off the countertop and stands defensively behind it. I recognize that stance, I've seen it too many times on domestic violence calls. Women who are beaten. They think they can defend themselves, but they can't or don't know how to, so they just brace themselves for the next swing. Her stance tells me there's history, and that hurts in a way I didn't anticipate. I tread lightly to her, my hands raising in defense. I'm not the one she should fear. I take her trembling shoulders in my hands and look her straight in the eye.

"Well, I just turned cop. You're being threatened Mya. So, tell me what you saw." I try to stay calm, to show her she can trust me, that I won't hurt her, but my instinct to protect her is coming through as pure fury.

"I don't know. Why do you care Cole? We barely know each other and one time at Styne's doesn't make you my protector. Just get out," she screams at me, but her screams are weak, her voice is trembling and her words, fragmented. Hearing her in such distress rips me in two. Mya's been hurt in the past, she's being hurt

now, and she doesn't trust me. This is not how it's supposed to play out; she is supposed to trust me. I'm the fucking good guy.

"*Mya.*" I say softly, trying again to calm her, to reassure her but—

"*Go!*" She screams out clear and forceful. This time I take notice. I take a step back extending my arms while still holding her shoulders. I look around and realize where I'm standing. I'm in *her* home demanding answers to questions I shouldn't be *officially* asking.

She looks up, her eyes demand my exit. She needs to feel safe and if me leaving makes her feel safe then I'll go. I release her, take a step back and shove my hands in my pockets. I look her over a last time before I turn and walk out her front door.

***

"*FUCK!!*" I punch the steering wheel. I punch it again and again. I'm angry that she lied. I don't know how to protect her if she doesn't tell me what is going on. I am angry that I'm not holding her anymore and that she just threw me out of her house. And worse, I'm disgusted with myself for fucking Paige and hurting Mya, a wound she doesn't know exists yet.

I look back at her front door hoping I'll see her coming down the steps. She isn't, and my fist hits the steering wheel again.

The truck is quiet, much like my apartment, but my thoughts are not. I feel like I am losing myself all over again. I haven't felt this much rage since I walked in on Paige. I was hurt by Paige because she was *mine,* she was my future. Mya is—Mya is a speeding ticket and so far, a minute of my life as compared to the life I had with Paige. But it's Mya. She's too important to me now. She's hurting and I can't help her. Some asshole is threatening her, calling her names and that alone makes my blood run hot.

***

I don't mean to be so rude when I arrive back at the station, but I breeze right by Carol as she says hello.

"Is he in, Carol?" I ask her curtly.

"Yes, Cole, he's in his office," even at this late hour she smiles brightly.

I let myself into the Captain's office without even the courtesy of knocking. His hand stops writing, and he looks at me over his glasses which have fallen down his nose. I see he's alone, so I shoot right off, only then noticing my brother seated in the corner dressed in his Friday night attire.

"Pop, she's involved. Someway she's mixed up with the Olden case. A weird coincidence, I'm sure, but I feel like the universe is trying to put pieces together for me. I'm not seeing clearly especially where she is concerned. I pull her over for speeding. The most memorable traffic stop, yes, but she was also frightened. Why? I continue pacing the floor as I outline the chain of events leading to this exact moment. Pop and my brother remain silent as they hear me out.

Now, a new lead brought me right to her fucking front door and she wasn't just frightened, she was terrified. She's the woman Bill saw behind his tree. Maybe the shots fired were meant for Mya? Did the shooter know she was there? He must have. I mean, she's being threatened. Pop, she's being threatened."

"Cole, calm down. The Olden case?" My father walks around from behind his desk. Dustin approaches me as well, and I remain motionless until both are standing in front of me.

"Do I have your attention now?" I say as I pull the note from my back pocket and hand it to them.

"How did you get this, Cole?" Dustin asks, his eyes the size of saucers.

"I just left there. I needed to know she is okay. I saw the note and asked her about it." I quickly clarify for him.

Pop slowly removes his glasses, pausing his movements and then continuing, *"Cole, this is serious. She needs a protective detail assigned to her. If she witnessed something and this note is legit then she needs protection."*

Dustin shouts a few orders to Carol, something about Dave and skipping tomorrow morning briefing. I collapse in the chair, finally feeling validated. My father sets his hand on my shoulder to comfort me as he acknowledges that Mya must be someone special.

"I care for her, Pop." I utter the words slowly and under my breath. He nods silently in confirmation.

My need to protect her goes beyond the irrational connection I feel with her. My body craves her. Every moment I've been with her makes me feel alive. If she's broken, I will fix her. If she's scared, I'll comfort her. It's the least I can do since somehow, she's filling the void Paige left behind; a void I thought I had to accept.

*****

Dave arrived the next morning frantically asking what the hell was going on. We proceed to fill him in on what I discovered about Mya and the threat she received. He shares what he learned from Bill, the nosey neighbor, and some of the pieces start to fit together. After questioning Bill and looking through binders of mug shots, Dave said he pointed out a handful of men who he recognized or who he thought could have been at the Olden's that night. Dave supplied us with a list of those names and Dustin hustles back to his desk to obtain backgrounds and cross reference those names with any other case files.

Finally, we may have something.

12

Mya

"Relax," he whispers into my ear from behind. His growly whisper liquefies my insides, my legs tremble as he peppers tiny kisses along the skin behind my ear. He drags his tongue down my neck to the tip of my shoulder and kisses it. I can't move. His body is pressed against mine. My breasts are pushed flat against the cold glass, causing my nipples to perk up. My body tenses again when his fingers slip between my cheeks and rubs past my asshole. *"Ah, I'll be there soon enough."*

He moans. His thick fingers slide lower and linger at my opening. *"Ah, you're wet, baby."*

***

"Mya hunny. You must get going. Trisha will be waiting."

My mom's voice pulls me from my erotic daydream as I stare into the full-length mirror in the spare bedroom. I haven't seen or heard from Cole since he found the threat. That was over two weeks ago. I cowered when he shouted at me and in response told him to leave. Whatever I thought or had hoped was building between us, is now a moot point. I wanted to believe that he shouted because he cared, because he must have felt what I was feeling, too. But he's made no attempt to contact me since that night. I've stayed away from Styne's even though Trisha continues to go every Friday to see Dustin.

My body aches for him, my mind constantly betraying me with daydreams of sexual fantasies. My nerves are so pent up I'm almost to the point of full explosion. Why couldn't I just tell him the truth? Tell him what I know or don't know about the Olden's. Tell him *how* I know the Olden's, but how do I do that? Do I just blurt out that their son used to beat the shit out of me? I barely knew them when I was dating their son. It was total

108

coincidence that I was even near their house that night. I shouldn't have kept any of it from him.

Coincidently, my mother called me shortly after that encounter with Cole, to see how the Missouri Holdings meeting went. It had been a while since I'd seen her, so I took time off from work to visit. It's been nice being here with her, keeping her company as she putters. We talk each night about Dad and Brody over a few glasses of wine.

My younger brother is finishing his second year of college. He's coming home for Christmas and it's all my mother can talk about—getting her baby's room ready. Brody won't stay to live but after our father died, he and I humor our mom and let her pamper us when the opportunity arises. This was my time. Though, my visit with her hasn't taken my mind off Cole it has taken my mind off the Olden shooting and scary black jeeps. She's all up to speed on recent events and even though she doesn't want me to go home alone, I promised her I had Cole's number and would use it if I needed to.

I promised Trisha I would be home for a closing contract signing, so I guess my three-week sabbatical is over. I gather up the last of my bags and throw them in the trunk of my car.

"Bye, mom, I'll call you in a few days." I pull her close for one more hug, one that'll need to last me until I can get back here again to visit.

"Goodbye hunny. Please keep Cole on speed dial and call me if you need anything."

"I promise." I assure her.

Exiting her driveway, I turned left onto the main road and head for home.

I keep the radio silent and barely crack the window. The whistling air mollifies me causing my thoughts to be inconsistent. I can't focus on any one thought. Work, Mom, Brody, contracts, Olden's, gunfire, threats, Cole, the list goes on and on.

I miss him. I miss the cowboy him, not the cop him. I miss the heat between us and the pleasure I become dizzy with when he's near me. I think about the firmness behind his kiss and how he once wrapped his hands around my throat. I didn't fear him; I wanted him. There was a mysterious darkness there that intrigued me, and still does.

Cole is safe. I know deep down he won't hurt me but the tone he used, the rage in his face, it all battles with my emotions from the past. The same fear that should scare me away is exactly what ignites the passion deep inside me and keeps me grounded.

I want to hear his voice. I connect the call and he answers the phone on the first ring. His tone is strained and the tentativeness in his voice is new. He's different;

different than any other time we've talked. I've been away, yes, but this is not the same Cole I'm used to conversing with. There's rustling in the background; he's distracted. His breathing is irregular, he sounds almost annoyed that I called. I become light-headed when I think I may have just interrupted *something with someone.*

"I'm sorry, Cole, I'll let you go. I shouldn't have called." He doesn't respond but I hear him sigh deeply. I hang up before he has a chance to say anything and my heart breaks a little.

I call Trisha next. She answered on the 2nd ring. *"Hey, you, are you heading home?"*

"Hey…yeah. Should be home in about twenty minutes. Want to come over?" I ask. Historically she would have already been at my house waiting with a bottle of wine, but it seems Dustin has swept her off her feet.

"I would, Hun, but I have Dustin here. He's cooking me dinner." Her voice drops to a whisper. *"He's finally asked me out on that fucking date."* she quips.

"Oh my God, Trisha, you are too much. I think I'm going to bed anyway; I'll see you in the morning."

Twenty-five minutes later I pull into the driveway. N. Campbell Street feels unusually quiet tonight. I've not been away long but its long enough to feel a bit disoriented now that I've arrived back home.

I take a moment to recall the last time I was here. After Cole kissed me and after seeing that damn note. I sat and stared at the floor sobbing after he walked out so suddenly. I wanted him to come back, but how could I expect him to come running back, to emotionally save me, after I just demanded he leave. Instead, I did the next best thing. I pulled my shit together and ran away to my mother's house.

Kicking off my sneakers, I drop my keys and bag at the door. I wander over to the refrigerator and pull a bottle of Pinot. As I fill the glass, I sift through the unopened mail Trisha collected in my absence. Most are accounting and beauty magazines, some credit card offers, and a plain white envelope very similar to the others I'd received.

"Fuck." My knees give out and I surrender my body to the chair behind me. I exhale slowly trying to keep my paranoia at bay. The same stale cigarette smell sours my stomach as I open the envelope. My face pales, and a wave a nausea boils to my throat.

I grasp at my chest becoming angrier and angrier as I spread the pictures out across the table. There must be over thirty photos of me. Most are within my proximity, my V neck shirt I wore to the Missouri meeting, me at Pins, at the gym. Several of me at the office, some of me here sitting on the couch. The images become more intimate, showing me sleeping, showering, and dressing. It's evidence that he's been following me, that he can get close to me, that I'm not alone. He knows every detail of my everyday routine. Where I'm going, what I'm doing, and where I work. I'm furious with myself. How did I let this happen? How did I let it get this bad, who is this person? The last picture steals my breath, a gun. The point of view sends a clear message. The barrel points directly at me with a blurry figure standing behind it. I begin to tremble as I read the word on the opposite side.

BANG BANG MYA

No sooner do I read the words do I hear a loud heavy thud outside my kitchen window. I open it slightly investigating the sound. *"Whore."* I hear the whispered vulgarity and then a clang of metal.

I'm easily startled from the loud noise and I drop my glass of wine shattering it on the floor, leaving small shards of crystal beneath me.

I'm not alone, and that realization is palpable.

I hurl myself down, stumbling to the floor, and crawl into the corner of the room. Small pieces of glass cut my skin leaving bloody streaks in my wake. I clutch the phone as if it is my safety net, a security blanket that'll hide me from whomever is outside.

I dial my mother but hang up. My mouth becomes dry and horse. My fear so tangible I'm choking on it. I dial his number before I know my fingers are pressing the buttons.

"Cole!" I send a blood curdling cry through the phone.

"Mya?"

"Cole, he's here!" I force the words out just before an outbreak of tears take over.

"Mya. Mya...Don't hang up the phone." He states it calmly and then repeats it again and again under hustled breathes and slamming doors. But it's the sound of his squealing tires that calms me, he's coming for me.

I say nothing, I can't say anything. I just sit and wait, gripping the phone with both hands to my ear, trembling around like a pebble on shaky ground.

"Keep breathing, Baby, I can hear you." His words are my lifeline, a reminder that he is on his way and I'm not truly alone. Time passes slowly, or so it seems.

The door handle rattles, and I jump. I wait. I don't move until I know it's Cole.

"Mya. Baby. Come open the door," he whispers his words through the phone. I stand slowly allowing the small shards of glass fall off my body.

I turn the lock and open the door just enough, so I can see him, so he can see me. It registers to him immediately that I'm terrified. My shuddering is involuntary at this point. He wraps me in his arms and holds me tight to his chest. He knows it's the only place my trembling will eventually subside.

"Jesus. Mya," he murmurs. *"You're okay now. I'm here,"* he hushes me, squeezing me tighter.

"Shut the door…" I struggle with the words, he isn't listening. *"Shut the door!"* I repeat almost screaming.

He finally complies, releasing me and clicking the door closed behind him. He turns back around slowly as if a light bulb has just gone off.

"Show me."

"Cole. I— "

"Mya, don't argue…show me." He puts his hand out demanding that I produce the tangible he knows exists.

He follows me into the kitchen, and I show him the spread of pictures on the table. I watch his face grow angry as he scans the photos. His jaw begins ticking and without looking away he reaches into his back pocket and retrieves his phone.

"Cap, the threats are back, and they've escalated." He pauses *"Yes, I'm staying here with her."* He hangs up and pushes his phone back into his jeans pocket.

"I never saw him. Cole, well, I saw him, kind of, but I didn't 'see' him. I couldn't pick him out of a line up, if that's what you're thinking. You think I know more than I do, but I don't. I don't know who this is, or what he wants. I—" I start to sob, losing control of all reality. Cole wraps his arms around me knowing I need him more than ever.

"Cole, I was just in the wrong place at the wrong time. I don't know anything, I swear." My voice rattles and my face falls into my hands. *"I don't want to be alone."*

"Then I'll stay," he whispers.

He holds me for as long as I need until my shaking stops. Once it has, he releases me, turns and begins pulling wine, bread, and jelly from the refrigerator.

"I'm starving, do you want a sandwich?"

"I, um. Okay," I stutter along surprised by his unexpected change in behavior.

"Sit," he says grinning and just like that, I'm safe. Cole is here and he's staying. He's making sandwiches trying to bring back some normalcy to the night. He pulls two wine glasses from the cupboard and sets them

down in front of me. Smirking, he points to the glasses with the knife as if telling me to start pouring. He smears peanut butter and jelly on some bread, shakes some chips from the bag and we sit quietly at the countertop drinking wine and eating our PB&J sandwiches.

It's quiet and still, it helps me focus in and listen as he takes each breath, trying not to stare as he chews each bite. In between my own bites I watch his chest rise and fall, daydreaming about resting my head there. He catches me looking at him and smirks.

"I caught you again." He quips.

I blush and try to think of something fast before shit gets awkward.

"I'm sorry. I was just thinking about your shoulder." I inquire casually. *"When we kissed, I touched you there and you flinched."*

"Bullet," he says coolly as he takes another bite of sandwich, as if its everyday he tells people he has a bullet wound. Dusting the crumbs from his hands, he rises from his chair and retrieves the broom and dustpan.

"What!?" I quickly counter on a cough covering my mouth with my napkin.

"I completed my tour, and this was my souvenir," he says tapping his left shoulder. *"A bad day in Iraq and I caught a bullet. A little nerve damage but it only hurts after it's been worked."*

"Worked?"

"You know, at the gym, chasing some asshole or sweeping a beautiful woman off her feet." We both cheekily grin as we explore one another trying to guess what the other's thinking. The butterflies in my belly start a full-on swarm as the anticipation rises.

"Listen, Cole, I'm sorry I called you. I tend to overreach. You can go now if you want too. I'll be fine."

He tips the dustpan into the trashcan and tiny pieces of glass jingle to the bottom.

"I don't want to."

He turns to me as if he has something important and troubling to say but instead, he takes my plate away and puts it in the sink. My heart's doing cartwheels watching him take matters into his own hands, watching him take control of my kitchen.

The room starts to feel hot as my lower half spirals from the sexual tension coursing between us. He reaches for my hand, encouraging me to stand up, and walks us to the living room. He spins me around and he secures his hands tightly around my waist. Our eyes lock as he walks me backwards into the wall. I'm not going anywhere now; I'm trapped. Our breathing is heavy, each breath is drawn out, silence is our catalyst to passion. He pulls my waist into what I know is his growing erection.

"I. Won't. Leave. You. Alone." He growls each word independently. *"So please don't ask me to."* Then he playfully places his hat on my head, which pushes my curls down flat against my face.

His fingertips spread out across my brow pushing the hair from my eyes. I lift my hands and rest them flat on his chest; that's his signal. He rests one arm above my head, steadying himself against the wall behind me. He lowers his head and brushes his lips against mine. They are are soft and moist, and I'm ravening for more than what he's giving me. My mouth opens and it begins.

Our tongues intertwine and battle for space between our lips. A kiss like this releases a moan from deep in my throat. My hums of pleasure and acceptance cause him to press in harder, taking my mouth as if it's the only thing happening in the world for him. His other hand comes up between our bodies and cups my breast. The pressure of his hand kneading me over my lace bra sends a lightning storm through my body. The friction makes my nipples taut giving him something to roll between his fingertips. He growls the most delicious groan into my mouth and our kiss becomes deeper still.

His hand disappears and then shows itself again with handcuffs. I look down at the silver metal and I'm rendered speechless, but the ache in my lower stomach intensifies, the same it did when he tightened his hands around my throat. Cole Styne is not Peter. I'm not scared of him, I won't be. I'm curious about his tendencies, his sex room and I wonder if he'll ever take me down there.

Before I can give it much more thought, I hear a clip and feel the cold hard metal tighten around my wrist. He trails his fingers down my other arm to my wrist and secures it into the cuff. I gaze up at him. I see the familiar darkness and dominancy I used to run from, but this is sexual. It is not born from anger…it's born from love, from passion, from someone who is good. My insides exploded with excitement at the revelation that Cole is starting to become *someone* to me.

He picks me up effortlessly, bringing my legs around his hips. He stands there for a moment as I lift my cuffed hands over his head. He walks us to the couch, sits down and helps me adjust until I'm straddling his lap. He slowly pulls me into him, tugging at my ass and pulling my center into his hardness. His lips part as desire drips from them and he finds my mouth again. He kisses me slowly and passionately, our tongues and lips never separating.

I start a subtle grind against his stiff cock, and as I do, he deliberately rips my pants so there's one less barrier between us. My desire for him, all of him, is scorching hot and I know I am finally going to get the release I've wanted since that first time in his gym. His touch is perfect and intimate, but I want more. My pussy is warm and wet and screaming to be penetrated. I want him to fill me, I want to feel the slow grind of our bodies as we explore all that we have been impeding.

"Mya, we shouldn't," he breathes into my mouth breaking our kiss. Not again!! With those words, my body and modesty shatter with embarrassment.

"Cole." His name from my lips is riddled with frustration. I'm fucking irritable.

"Mya, I can't." He lifts my arms up over his head, removes the cuffs and throws them aside. He picks me up just enough to remove me from his lap and lowers me down beside him. What the fuck? I straightened myself out, pull a blanket over my lap since there's now a giant hole in the crotch of my pants. I tentatively remove the hat he had placed on my head, realizing that our moment of dress up and role play is over.

"Are you married or something. Do you have a girlfriend?" I begin drilling him for answers as to why he continues to stop the insanely hot sex we have yet to have.

"No, baby, no. I, well, a fiancé, but it's over…has been for months. But…you have a lot going on. I'm an officer

on the case, where you have a lot going on and—Paige is back and she's pregnant."

Silence deafens the air. The word fiancé and pregnant pull any air I have left out of my body. I'm devastated and broken. There's nothing else to say, and just like that, it's over.

"Oh. Okay." I clear my throat, feeling as though I'm choking on the words. I'm angry that he's led me on; he used me for some quick fix and lied to me. I'm completely humiliated. He needs to go. Now. I say nothing more as I stand holding the blanket around my waste. I make my way to my bedroom, knowing he'll be going soon. I pass the kitchen table glancing at thirty different reasons why he should stay.

"Mya." He whispers my name almost apologetically.

"I heard you Cole."

I'm wounded by the distance he's just put between us. I continue to walk away shaking with humiliation. My modesty shot especially since I'm still hiding the huge hole in my pants. How could I be so stupid? I thought he liked me. I've been nothing but a play toy for him, a distraction while his fiancé was away. I'm a fool.

I look back at him before I reach my bedroom. He's sitting on the couch, his head hangs heavily in his hands, his knees bearing most of his weight. He looks miserable and broken. He sits for a while listening to my quiet sobs as if it's his punishment. After he's heard enough, he stands and walks out, saying nothing, leaving nothing, but me alone with a threat outside.

***

I wake with a start. *"Shit! I'm going to be late."*

I hurry myself through a shower and dress. I choose the grey pinstripe pencil suit with black stilettos boots. I pin my hair up in a messy up do—Trisha and my partnership contract closes today.

I open my bedroom door, he's still gone. Not that I expect him to be back, but the bareness of the living room stings after such a hot make out session. I run through the details Dustin told Trisha and she told me that night. Cole's fiancé who cheated on him, came back to him crying. They banged and now she's having his baby. Bing, Bang, Boom, I have no claim on him, he was never mine to begin with. What else is there to think about? Cole Styne belongs to someone else. I allowed myself three whole days to cry over him.

I grab my bag and keys, check my lipstick one last time in the hallway mirror and hustle out the door, forgetting completely about the threat that could lie past it.

I want to get this day started and over with.

***

"Trisha, are the senior partners ready?" I inquire as I enter the building.

"Ready and waiting," she responds, holding the conference door open for me.

"Good." I dig deep down for my best smile, flirtatious but professional, as I greet the firm's management team. Today is our last day as executive accountants. We will transfer our clients to the new blood and move our offices to the senior suite.

When all parties have signed the contract, they present us with our partnership agreements, keys to our new offices, and large bonus checks. The zeros have Trisha's eyes seeing beach vacations and martinis in France.

The rest of my afternoon is sprinkled with low level contract signing and spreadsheets. Transferring files and accounts and meeting with some clients who want their latest numbers crunched, making sure their retirement plans are safe and intact.

Trisha pops her head into my office pretty much every hour to be sure I haven't backed out of our celebratory drink at Styne's. She and Dustin have become serious, but I fear a run in with Cole or his returned fiancé. I find myself wondering what she looks like. Does he kiss her or touch her the same way he does me?

"Don't even ask, I'm going." I say annoyingly as she pops her head into my office again, the office I'm trying to pack up and move. I place another framed picture into the box. Most I've decided to take home rather than to my new office. I hesitate when I start to pack the Missouri Holdings picture with Trisha and me. The day I wore my V-neck shirt; the day *he* followed me.

I've only thought about the latest package of pictures a few times and nothing has been delivered to my house since. I've been more distracted with the delicious tingle between my thighs that reminds me of Cole and our steamy encounters. Regardless of the world exploding news that came after the last encounter, the thought of Cole Styne still makes me horny as hell.

I see Trisha lingering outside my office and before she can get a word out, my hand flies up to shut her up.

"Bitch, I'm going, stop asking,"

"YES!!!" she cheers skipping down the hall. I roll my eyes at my deliriously elated friend.

Like I said, I can not wait to get this day over with.

***

"Come on girl. He's here. I see his car."

125

Trisha celebrates as we exit the cab knowing that Dustin is inside waiting for her. She takes my hand and pulls me excitedly up the steps and through the front doors of Styne's. We check our coats and Dustin greets us on the other side of the saloon doors, champagne in hand.

"Ladies. Congratulations on becoming millionaires," he cheers offering us each a kiss on the cheek as we clink our glasses together.

It's obvious I'm a third wheel since Dustin and Trisha are already gooey eyed over each other and heading to wherever it is they go.

I find myself sitting in an empty chair adjacent to the stage where I can easily see Cole, but he'd have a hard time seeing me. But he's there, with his guitar, singing a country song that has my foot tapping to the beat. His husky voice and the bounce of his knee is giving me all the feels in all the right places. I begin daydreaming about my cuffed hands and how wide open I was straddling his lap; our deep kiss, and how amazing it felt grinding into his erection. Oh, how I wanted so much more than that. Watching him play now and move to the music reignites that tingle between my folds.

"Congratulations, Love." I sit motionless. I recognize the voice. The past now ringing in my ears like a loud emergency horn. I turn slowly in my seat to face the man speaking but don't offer him even a smile.

"Peter." I say tentatively, internally breathing in and out, chanting to myself that I'm okay. Thank you, therapy. Plus, Cole is nearby. I'm okay. I stay seated, hoping he'll just go away. If I stand, he'll see my shaking frame and know he's gotten to me. But I'm not seated long before I'm pulled up by my arm and forced into an embrace. A fake hug, one that's for show.

"How am I? How are you? I heard you landed a huge contract. That's amazing." He smiles that smile that was always meant for me. In the beginning of course, he was the one to calm and comfort me. That was until he started drinking and his fists replaced his words. He can't keep this artificial conversation going long, not in such a public place. I make the most of his pause and attempt my escape. I make my way to the bar hoping someone will see my uncomfortableness around him.

"Thank you, Peter. What are you doing here, I haven't seen you in years?" I ask trying to move the awkward conversation along.

Peering around to find Wyatt is out of earshot, Peter takes my hand firmly into his and leans down to my ear.

"Ohh Mya. You know you've seen me because I've seen you."

My face turns hot as he continues squeezing my hand, my usual warning not to make a scene. He starts to trace his hand up my arm and reaches for my cheek.

"Peter," I blurt out his name taking a huge step back missing his hand by an inch.

"You know I don't like it when you pull away." he says just under his breath, forcing a smile and this time aggressively grabbing my arm. *"I miss you, Mya."*

"Peter, let go." I try a little harder to pull away but it's no use; he's much stronger than I am. I can smell the stale beer and tobacco on his breath, and it sickens my stomach. I instinctively try to pull free, but he grips me harder.

"Ouch, Peter," I wince.

I hadn't noticed the music stop until his voice boomed and echoed through the Tavern.

"The lady said to let her go." Cole steps in-between us ripping me from Peter's grasp. His eyes are lethal, and his jaw is ticking rapidly. He sees red and I'm pretty sure he's going to kill Peter.

"Cole, it's fine, he's my ex." I try to explain quietly and calmly. It did no good; my clarification of who the man was has only fueled Cole's wrath.

"Cole." I try again to get his attention by taking his hand. The slight graze of my fingertips must have been a warning sign because he instead possessively grabs for mine and holds our intertwined hands behind his back.

"You've hit her haven't you, you fucking coward? Try it again and I'll fucking kill you" Cole explodes with rage. I hide behind him as a shield, as he instigates Peter.

Peter puffs out his chest realizing someone knows about his past discretions and the two are in a draw. I've seen Cole angry, hell he's been angry with me but right now he looks murderous.

"Mya, Love, call me…"

"Don't!" Cole steps forward as if tempting Peter to finish the sentence. Peter smiles, surrenders, and walks away.

Only after he's sure Peter has gone; Cole turns to me, his eyes burning with rage and desire in equal parts. I glare at him seeking clarification to what he's thinking, but his eyes tell all. He knows. He knows I've been mistreated. He's witnessed my recoiling and the fear that surrounds me when he's angry. He knows that Peter is an ex, Cole has put the two pieces together on his own. He pulls me through the Tavern, through the doors of the bar and into a back room. He pushes me against the wall and takes my mouth hard.

"Cole, stop." I try to get a word in.

"You should've been loved Mya, not hit. Let me love you." He pants breathlessly.

His hand finds the hem of my skirt. His fingertips dig into my inner thigh almost painfully. He raises my leg and pulls it over his hip, opening my center up wider. I can feel the hardness of his cock pushing against me, teasing my entrance. He holds my leg with one hand and his other yanks my underwear to the side. His fingers slide easily through my folds; I'm already wet and he can feel it too as he rubs my pussy.

I don't want him to stop this, but I must. I was just confronted by the man who used to beat me, now I'm being groped by a man who can't stop touching me. The feelings are so foreign to each other, so opposite, like good and evil. It has my head spinning with emotions as raw as an open wound. I can't get a word spoken before he's muffled them with a forceful kiss.

With a final attempt to tell him to stop, he's breaches my warm wet center with his fingers, and he begins pumping them in and out. My mouth opens wide and my head falls back against the wall in response to his assault.

"Cole. Stop, we can't do this. You said you can't do this," I say almost out of breath as he continues to circle and thrust his fingers into me. He's in a zone. I can barely make out the faint words he's muttering with each push of his fingers.

"Cole." I stress and push him away trying to get my message across.

"I know what I said, Mya. But I can't," he pleads and then pauses slowing his pace down. The reality of what is transpiring sets in and he releases my leg. He presses his forehead into mine and wraps his hands around my ribs, his thumbs cupped just under by breasts. His face dips into my neck; tenderly kissing and suckling my skin. He brings his hands up and grabs a fistful of hair, pulling slightly so my head is pulled back and off to the side exposing more of my neck.

His growl tells me he can't stop, that he doesn't want to. He wants me as much as I *need* him.

"Mya, tell me you don't want this, and I'll stop."

My heart is already breaking. I pinch my eyes closed readying myself for what I'm about to say.

"I don't want this."

He stops immediately, pushing his weight from me and backing away. He looks like I just ripped his heart from his chest, like he's a boy and I just murdered his puppy.

"Why do you look so destroyed Cole?" My angry question renders him speechless. He says nothing for a moment then tries to turn the situation on me.

"Who was that guy, Mya? I saw how he was with you; he's hit you once hasn't he?"

"I wish it were only once Cole. But he's an ex. My ex. What does it matter anyway? What do you want from me? Your fiancé is back, she's having your baby, so what the fuck are you doing here with me?" I scream angrily through my tears.

I straighten myself out and storm away having nothing more to say. Each step taking me further from the first good man who's come into my life in years.

***

I spend few minutes in the ladies' room trying to gather myself together. I fix my hair and lipstick, so I won't appear as though I was just manhandled. A few minutes turn to several minutes after a fit of rage and eruption of tears. Eventually, I gain the courage to walk back out there. Thankfully, Peter is gone and has not returned. The place is in the full Friday night swing. I just want to go home.

I look over to Trisha and find her dancing with Dustin. She won't be ready to leave for some time. I return to my barstool close to Wyatt who is none the wiser of all that just transpired. I sit stunned and dazed, feeling deliciously violated.

"Can I get another, please?" I yell down to Wyatt, waving my empty bottle.

13

Cole

She didn't leave. Thank god, she didn't leave. She came back to the bar and thankfully close to Wyatt.

My singing is shit. My playing even worse with my fingers still damp from her arousal. I was murderous watching as she tried to free herself from her ex. I knew he was the one who had hit her. I could tell by her body language, and his. I had to change that. I saved her from that prick and at the same time, I was so turned on by the fact that she even needed saving. I *had* to be with her again. But then, she said no. My fingers were knuckle deep in her pussy when she said she didn't want it. What could I do?

Another hour passes and I've watched her down drink after drink. Now there's this asshole. He's keeping his distance but he's inching his way closer to her. He has his hand around the back of her stool when Wyatt brings her another drink. Fuck, she doesn't even notice his movements. I'm getting irate watching this guy move in on my girl.

Before I know it, my song is over. I cradle my guitar in its stand and I'm off the stage in a flash. I interject myself into their conversation, standing right in front of her shoving the new guy away and demanding her attention. Her eyes fly up to mine, and just like that our quarrel is over, our hunger is palpable, we're craving each other.

"Are you sober?"

"Yes." An immediate response? She might just be. Her eyes are begging for me to take her.

"Good." I press my palm against her face, push her hair behind her ear, and whisper *"because I'm going to fuck you now."*

She squeals in delight as I lift her off her feet and throw her over my shoulder. The place goes wild with cheers at my declaration of affection.

"Cole...put me down." I ignore her pleads and give her a firm whack on her ass. *"Ouch,"* she cries out through her laughter.

I carry her upstairs to my apartment as her requests to put her down continue.

I sit her ass on the kitchen counter and spread her legs open with a little more force than I intended. She gasps. I step in between them as her hands come up circles around my neck.

"Please don't push me away. Not again," she says with a shaky voice as the air crackles between us.

We look into each other's eyes knowing that this is our moment, we are both going to let this happen. We have let go of all the "no's," and will finally surrender to the lure that keeps bringing us together. Paige is not here; her ex is no longer a problem and I want her, and she wants me. This is our time to feel fully and completely what we've wanted to feel since the start.

I hold her wrists lightly in my hands and pull her arms above her head.

"Leave them," I command, and she obeys like a good girl. I slip her dress over her head exposing her perfect round tits, cradled inside plush lace. I skim her silky skin with my lips, peppering her with kisses. *"You're fucking beautiful, Mya."*

I find her left breast and I begin kissing, pulling and lapping at her skin with my mouth. She lets go of a moan that has my cock twitching and begging to be inside her. She spreads her fingers through my hair, tugging, and pushing my face tighter into her breast. My single fingertip pulls her bra down just enough allowing her right nipple to pop free. I bite and lick and tug at it with my mouth. I leave that nipple to release the other. Her bare mounds are the perfect size and shape. I stand upright, watching as she's coming undone before me. My hands set a course from her knee to her ass, pulling her into my hardness. She throws her head back and pushes her chest out. My mouth finds her other breast and I repeat the same routine, licking and tugging at her nipple with my mouth. Her moans are increasing at a steady rate and I start licking with fuller strokes as I lap up the sweat from her skin.

"I want to see you," I growl. I can feel her wetness through her underwear, and I know she's ready. I pull them to the side. *"Look at me,"* my tone demands her eyes and just as she looks at me, I push my cock into her. I watch as her eyes widen, and her mouth fall open. I still myself and I can feel her tiny muscles tighten around me begging for more.

"Cole." She breathlessly mutters my name and it's my undoing. I pull out, teasing her hole with the tip and then drive myself into her again. She cries out and pulls herself up onto the countertop as she anticipates my forceful thrusts. I pick her up, cock still inside, and I carry her to the bedroom. I lay her down; I take my time, focusing on every inch of our skin that is touching as I try to absorb every drop of her that's spilling over.

She's coming apart; she throws her arms above her head. *"I want you."* She whispers. I gingerly pull myself up and position myself above her. I position myself at her center and with only a slight move of my hips, I push into her. My pace increasing with her acceptance apparent.

"Open your eyes, Mya." As she does, I pump a few more times before swiftly turning us over so she's on top straddling me.

Our new position pushes the full length of my cock into of her. Her erotic sigh almost puts me over the edge. She relaxes and begins circling her perfect figure on top of my dick; I reach the point of no return.

"I don't want to come yet baby. I want to enjoy this." She isn't listening. She is riding and grinding down on me, throwing her head back and releasing whimpers with each rotation.

"Cole, I'm going to come," she looks down at me timid and shy.

"It's okay, baby, let go," and she does. The sound of her climax makes me want to be even deeper, I am already fucking balls deep, but I sit up pushing my hard cock in deeper still. Her orgasm intensifies and echoes through the apartment. The sight of her coming is enough for me to find my own release. I braced myself with one arm behind me and hold her around the waist with the other. My cum threads out of me with each thrust and I bury my face in her breasts.

She rests her cheek on top of my head and releases an exhausted sigh. I smile, knowing she feels as sated as I do. Together, we ride the wave of our orgasms, enjoying every aftershock of pleasure that's delivered. We steady our breathing, until our breathing is in sync.

***

I look toward the window. It's still dark. I bring my hand up to Mya's forehead and trace it with my fingertips. I can feel her breathing steadily, as she's wrapped in my arms. It's the safest place for her, the only place I want her to be. The only place *I* want to be. She stirs a little and repositions her arm across my chest; circling her finger on my skin as she sleeps. In this moment I realize I've fallen in love with Mya Dylan. I steady my own breathing as to not wake her. She needs to rest.

14

Mya

My eyes flutter open. I'm paralyzed as I take in my surroundings. Where am I? Coles' place? Oh god, what have I done. Oh my god, what if she comes home? What is he doing? My paranoia shows itself. Cole, his fiancé, baby, Peter, my memory catches up as I remember all of what happened last night.

"*Morning, baby.*" His voice is deep and enriching. I look over and find him freshly showered, shirtless, barefoot in only his jeans. His muscles make my lady parts sing, those same muscles comforted me *and* fucked me last night. The last twelve hours, now a continuous loop in my mind like a horrible song on repeat.

I fly out of the bed and dress quickly, ignoring any attempt he's making at trying to stop me. He can't do this. He can't welcome home his fiancé who is pregnant and then fuck me on the side. I wanted him last night, of course I did. This crazy alluring attraction and passion between us has been caged for weeks, it needed to be let out. I had him and now what, I'm his mistress? I'm boiling mad. I walk up to him and I did something I never in a million years thought I'd have the courage to do. I slap him, hard across the face and he stands there, solid, accepting the blow as if he knows what it is for.

"You can't do this, Cole. We can't do this!" I yell.

"Mya, I've fallen in love—."

"Don't. Cole." I stop him. Shoving my hand in his face before he finishes that stupid sentence. He cannot love me. He can't love me and have a baby on the way with another woman. I want to slap him again, but my hand still hurts from round one. All my emotional barriers break down and I spew out all my own drama.

"My father left me when I was a child, Cole. I know what it's like to feel abandoned. You can't do that to

your baby. I was lucky enough to have my dad— my stepfather, for many years before he died. But you, Cole…you're still here and you have a chosen to stay. So, stay and let me go."

I'm sure my words have engrained themselves because I walk away, and he does nothing to try to stop me.

The moment was raw, but it was the truth, my truth.

I hustle down the steps knowing he'll be after me soon. The Tavern is quiet this morning yet memories of last night are appearing like ghosts. It's haunting.

It is early morning and it had snowed last night. I don't wait for my car to warm up. I don't want to chance him coming after me. I pull out of the Tavern's parking lot, my tires sliding and skidding through the slippery snow. I can barely see through my tears let alone my windshield. I don't see the headlights coming until it's almost too late, I turn the wheel so hard I just about veer off the road.

"Bitch…get out of my way!" I scream to the driver.

A petite woman eyes me through her side window, her mouth gaped open in surprise. She slams on her breaks hoping I'll do the same, but I keep driving. I ignore my phones infuriatingly buzzing knowing its him and I know Cole's fiancé has just arrived home.

Two Weeks Later

"Ok, I'll meet you there." I hang up the phone tossing it on the bed and continue to get ready for the day. Trisha's cleared her Saturday so she and I can go to Pins for a well-deserved mani-pedi and overdue girl-talk.

It's been two weeks since I fucked Cole or he fucked me, whatever it was exactly; it happened. I hate saying it like that because it was more than fucking. It was emotional, raw and intimate. I hadn't told Trisha about it yet, work has been busy, and we just haven't had a minute to catch up. I've spent the last two weeks trying to maintain my normal routine but never forgetting there is someone there, watching and preying on me. I work late hours to keep busy and when I am out of the office, I'm more vigilant than ever before.

Today though, I can relax, at least for a few hours. I'm going to tell Trisha everything today.

There was once a time I had promised her I'd never talk about Peter, but she must know he's in town. She had only met him a few times at the very beginning of our relationship when we'd come to Lorry Springs to visit. Nonetheless, as our nails are getting painted, I walk her through the intensity of the Peter encounter at Styne's and how Cole went all primal. All of which she missed because she and Dustin had disappeared somewhere. She's not surprised that Cole and I satisfied our sexual need for each other, *"That shit needed to happen for both of your sakes,"* she quips.

Over the next hour she tells me about Dustin and how she's finally found her match, and that was *before* she realized she was pregnant.

"Wait. You're PREGNANT!?" I gape at her; did I hear that right. She's won the trophy for the most mind exploding news feed. She's grinning from ear to ear. *"I love him,"* she says. *"It must have happened shortly after we met. Not ideal but we are both ecstatic over it."* She continues.

I'm happy for my best friend and I suppose with this news and our promotions we have officially entered the next phase of adulthood.

She and Dustin hadn't told her parents yet, they are planning on some big Christmas surprise. *"Cole knows, though."* She states simply as if to test my reaction to his name. She knows as well as I that it is over with Cole. She had been the one to tell me about Paige and the baby in the first place.

We leave the salon section of Pins with our nails well-manicured and polished. We grab a chair and order our usual lattes and strawberry pastries, the large one, with the big dollop of fresh fruit in the middle and sweet icing ribbon on top. Yum! After thirty minutes she orders a second and we pick at it with our forks. It gives us something to do while I tell her everything about the threats that have been sent to me, the weird cars, the black jeep, and Cole's protective nature. Saying it all out loud is overwhelming and makes the fear real again. If Cole can't be a part of my life anymore, I need someone else to know about the threats.

"Jesus, Mya, I had no idea." She rests her hand on mine and looks at me with empathy and sorrow. Though, she's become savvy about bringing me back to the here and now, she now understands why I will pause and check my surroundings. She apologizes for not knowing. I don't blame her; she had no idea nor would she.

Three hours later, with pretty nails and our bellies full of pastries, we set out of Pins. Though we had planned to separate at this point, Trisha decides to extend our visit. My guess, she doesn't want me to be alone. I love her.

"I see it." I look over Trisha's shoulder and I see the black jeep that has been taunting me for weeks.

"Trisha. He's here," I say just above a whisper riddled with debilitating terror. *"It's him."* My voice rattles and Trisha's eyes go wide at my sudden onset of fear.

"Wow, this is bad. Act normal, Hun." She digs through her purse, pretending as though she is laughing

and carrying on a conversation with me. I lean on her for strength, to keep my trepidation away. I pick up her subtle hint and try to appear as though nothing unusual is happening. She pops a stick of gum in her mouth with one hand and pulls her phone out with the other. She pretends to show me pictures on her phone and rubs her belly, still smiling and carrying on as if nothing is happening. All the while she is whispering words of comfort and encouragement. *It'll be okay. I'm getting help. It's fine.*

There are no pictures on her phone. She's texting Dustin and within minutes, and although I don't see him, she assures me that he's arrived. He's here in an unmarked patrol car and has parked just around the corner. He steps out from the alleyway as does Cole.

"Cole..." I whisper questioningly.

Neither of them acknowledges our presence, they're cops and their acting like it.

Dustin turns abruptly and starts toward the jeep. He puts his hand to his back, pushing his jacket away, exposing his gun. He grips it with one hand as he stalks toward the jeep. Cole matches his brother's swift movements and grips his own gun. They're stealthy but still tread heavily toward the jeep. Dustin rounds the driver side window with his gun drawn. Cole draws his gun but is clipped in the arm when the passenger side door flies opened.

The jeep suddenly speeds off and Dustin fires a few shots at the tires, missing.   Cole shoots and punctures the front tire causing the jeep swerve. It's is now barreling straight toward Trisha and me.

"*Cole!*" I scream for him, but he ignores my cry for help. He's mouthing letters and numbers trying to memorize the plates.

As if in a movie the moment slows to a crawl. My life, past and future flashes as the jeep inches closer to me. The windows are tinted but I can make out someone watching me out the side window. For a split second my gaze is drawn to the face peering out the front windshield. His stare is cold and lethal. My body is suddenly yanked backwards away from the speeding vehicle. The jeep deviates and turns down a side road.

"*Are you okay, miss?*" the stranger asks has he straightens himself out but I unable to respond.

"*She's fine,*" Trisha replies for me as she types vigorously into her phone. "*Come on, let's get you out of here.*"

She put me in my coupe and buckles my seat belt. I'm paralyzed and in shock from my near-death experience. I see Cole watching as Trisha buckles me in. I want to go talk to him, but Trisha speeds off.

"*I need to see him, Trisha.*" I yell.

"Not right now you don't." She snaps. Within a few turns, I know from my surroundings where we're headed.

"Trisha. No. I can't go to the police."

"Mya, we're banging the police!" She howls at me. She pauses and then speaks again a little calmer. *"I just mean, Dustin said you have to give a statement."* She lays her hand on my trembling knee.

My ear-piercing cell phone startles us both. She answers on my hands free and his voice booms through. *"Where are you now?"*

"Cole, he'll kill me if I go to the police." I speak right up in response.

"Mya, you're going. Don't argue. His voice responds. *You said you don't know anything, right baby? Once this asshole knows that maybe he'll leave you alone."*

I try again...*But Cole—"*

"Mya, shut up!"

I surrender.

15

Cole

That afternoon, Pop listened to Mya's story. How she knew the Olden's and where she was the night of the shooting. He agreed that she didn't know enough to be threatened but because this man didn't know that, he remained a threat to her.

Trisha, Dustin, and I stay with her for hours into the night. We order pizza and Dave went out to fetch us some beers. It's going to be a long night.

The binders are large, heavy, and have hundreds of mug shots of assholes from years past. Mya picks out a handful of faces she thought could have been the men in the black jeep. Trisha thinks she got a better look of the person in the passenger side once the door flew open.

I remain at Mya's side trying to calm her and remind her that I am the good guy. I want, no, need to kiss her, touch and hold her, but she won't let me. She pulls away at every attempt I make to get close to her. After a while, I settle for just being in her vicinity, close enough to smell her peach shampoo and hear the rhythm of her breathing.

I ignore my phone the few times Paige calls. I try to silence it before it causes a problem, but even on vibrate, Mya knows it is her. She glares fault at me as if I am intentionally making the goddamn thing ring. As if each ring is a knife stabbing her in the back repeatedly. I can see the pain in her face, her saddened eyes and it's breaking me down slowly.

"You recognize him? You keep coming back to Patrick." Dustin asks with urgency tapping his finger on a mugshot picture, his tone interrogative.

"He just reminds me of the man who killed my father. My stepfather." She clarifies looking over to me. I already knew her father left her and that her stepfather is the only man she ever called dad, but still it gave her a reason to look at me. I gaze into her eyes for the few

seconds she gives me, but it isn't long enough to tell her all I need to.

"How so, Mya?" Trisha asks, interrupting my wordless pronouncement of how in love I am with Mya.

"My dad had just picked me up from a party. A drunk driver came across the intersection. He caused a huge pile up but before the police or EMTs could get there he got back into his car and left the scene; probably seeing what he had caused."

"If you ask me, he looks a lot like that asshole ex of yours." Trisha's comparison to Peter piques my interest, but my brother is still fixed on the drunk driver.

"Did you ever give a statement? How long ago was this?" Dustin's persistence is heading for full on interrogation. I swiftly stand up from my chair, taking notice of my brother's keen attention to detail. Something's up. I rest my hand on his shoulder *strongly* encouraging him to ease up off my girl. He swipes my hand away and dives right into the next question. *"Mya, Cole said you were at the Olden's? Is that right?"* Trisha and Mya eye each other. Shits about to get interesting.

"Cole." Dustin leaves the office, nodding to me to follow. He's animated, alert and marches straight towards the Captain's office. After giving them a

reassuring nod, I leave the girls to sift through the binders. He has raised their concern.

"Pop! We have a break." Dustin roars into Dad's office outlining, what he seems to think, are the last pieces to the puzzle.

He's pacing vigorously back and forth, "T""ing his right hand into his left palm, as he outlines each piece of evidence specifically.

"Mya's stepfather died as a result of that pile up on route 10. You were away on tour, Cole, you don't know this case." He pauses briefly to clarify. *"But Mya was there, and she may have just recognized Patrick Sutton as the drunk driver. But back then, Patrick Sutton was a disturbed kid scared and ran away when he saw what he did. Fast forward. Mya is the woman Bill saw behind his tree, right? Even though he says she didn't get a good look, Bill picked Patrick as one of the possible mugs from the shooting. This is too much of a coincidence. What's Sutton's background, what's his connection with the Oldens?"*

I interject with what I know. *"I know Peter Olden, the Olden's son, he's bad news. He did a stint for sexual assault and battery when he was 22." That would have been right around the time of the Route 10 pile up."*

Captain roars at the possibility of solving both the Olden case and a years-old drunk driving case. *"Mya*

***

At Styne's that Friday night I can barely focus. I am playing, singing hit after hit waiting impatiently for her to arrive. I know she's being followed by the PD and she's been instructed to act as if they aren't around. Dustin and I have been working tirelessly all week to piece the stories together. After being released from prison, Peter left and never returned to Lorry Springs. He met Mya in a neighboring city and became fixated on the fact they were from the same town. Dustin dug up the cold case and identified the name associated to the rental car was by P Sutton. He's a ghost; no records of him or the name after the pile up. If Bill and Mya picked out Patrick Suttons mug, then he's someone of interest. Someone I want to meet. There's an APB out on Patrick now but a week out from the incident at Pins and the trail is running cold. We can't locate him, and we know Peter is hanging around town for his mother, though Angel and Brad deny him visiting.

Knowing she's being tailed by the PD puts me a little at ease, she just needs to get here to Styne's and have a good time. Forget about all her troubles. I need to see her and see for myself that she is okay. My mind is running away with me thinking about all the "what if's",

152

right up until she breezes through the doors. God, she is as beautiful as ever.

I play and watch as she makes her way around the Tavern and I'm taken back to the first time I saw her here. And as if she can feel my yearning for her and she turns and waves. She doesn't offer anything more, not a smile or a kiss in my direction, I don't even get a playful wink, just a wave.

Mya has put distance between us; a physical and emotional barrier that so far, I can't tear down. She won't answer my calls, my texts, and Trisha refuses to get involved. I know the PD will protect her but I'm not with her, so I have no control over her wellbeing, personally or professionally. Each day is slow and agonizing; wishing I could see her and touch her again.

I love her and she won't let me say it. I have a baby on the way, but does that mean my future must be with Paige? Paige has made herself very comfortable in my apartment, moving her stuff back in as if she never left. She's acting as though nothing happened, but for me, the awkwardness and resentment remain very present.

The uncomfortableness makes her overcompensate and she's become annoying as fuck.

I watch my girl settle herself at the bar. Her slim legs cross and her arms settle on the counter clutching her wallet. She's content. Within moments, Paige approaches her. Fuck, I forgot Paige was helping Wyatt tonight. He's out at his grandson's rodeo competition and won't be back for another little while. Paige fetches Mya a beer and opens it for her. I watch as the two women chat for a few moments. To anyone else it would be a bartender and a patron conversing about current headlines, but I know better. My blood boils when I see Paige place her hand across her belly, patting it lightly, and pointing to me.

She's talking to Mya about the baby, about me! My eyes grow sympathetically wide and my throat closes on me when Mya turns herself on the stool. Her eyes find me. They are fixed on me, shooting daggers as she takes a forcible sip of her beer. She's furious, but worse, she's uncomfortable. She nor I can do anything about it. She can't get up after *that* encounter with Paige and not be obvious about it. I did not fucking remember that Paige was helping tonight. Fuck.

I'm might be on stage, but I'm not useless. I can sing to her. I can stand here and try to keep her attention. To tell her through my songs, my singing, and through the look in my eye, that I wish *it* were different. That I know she can't deal with Paige right now; *Mya, baby I know. I want you and only you; I love you.*

But some drunk fucker keeps standing in my way, her attention stolen from me time after time making it difficult to say what I need to say.

Wyatt returns and relieves Paige of duty. She retires upstairs, and suddenly I'm free. Free to love Mya openly and without Paige's interference but I've already lost her to this asshole. He is touching her and soothing her, trying to cheer her up. I look around for Dustin, but he and Trisha are gone. The PD security is debriefing and swapping shifts so for the moment she's alone. I stand behind my guitar and sing, and I watch as this man's arms fall all over my girl, and worst yet, she's enjoying it. She's laughing and is having a good time. The PD wouldn't intervene now anyway, not if she's visibly having a good time and not asking for assistance.

This ass is twisting his fingers through her brown hair and tapping, playfully on her knee. My next ten years begin to flash through my mind. I imagine Mya and Paige and my unborn child, what the fuck am I supposed to do?

She's nuzzling into his arm now, she's drunk. She's clearly unable to make any rational decisions. The thought of her in someone else's arms, inebriated, and out of control, curdles my blood and makes me want to spit nails. I try to catch Wyatt's attention, so he will stop serving her. It's no use. The place is busy tonight. The staff is distracted and can barely keep up with the number of people coming and going.

Mya might not think she is mine, not with Paige upstairs, but I love her, and I'm annoyed as fuck watching someone else have their hands on her.

16

Mya

I can't keep it together. It is so infuriating watching Cole as he sings to me. Does he know I just met his precious Paige and baby? Fucking hell, he knows, he watched it all happen. Every part of me that was falling in love with Cole Styne is shattering piece by piece. He was hers first. I watched her rub small circles on her stomach. I became nauseous and it really hit me that it is Cole's baby in there. I could barely taste or swallow the beer she handed me.

He told me he couldn't be with me, or I told him, either way, it needed to be over. We couldn't continue giving into our emotions, regardless of the passion that draws us to one another.

Now the thought of her upstairs is breaking me down slowly. I picture her lying out on the couch, bundled in his clothes, nursing her morning sickness. He should be up there with her and not down here with me, singing and giving me these sympathetic glances. We can no longer have a future whether he wants the one that is waiting for him or not. I know how that baby will grow up without a father, abandoned and unloved as I did. At least until my mother married my stepfather.

With my heart tearing, and my feelings already shattered, I can't hold back the tears any longer. I look around Styne's Tavern and unexpectedly feel out of place.

This is Cole's bar; it's his apartment upstairs. I'm the new girl. Everyone probably knew and loved Paige back when they were together. They are probably thrilled that she's back. I wipe my face. I need to leave before I completely splinter with humiliation. As I stand to leave as a man approaches me asking if I'm alright. He has a sweet smile; he's tall, thin and dresses in an inexpensive suit. He has some facial hair and a baseball cap on. His hands, especially his fingers, scream mechanic. He mentions having a mutual friend, and he offers to buy me a drink, so I accept. He puts his arm around me, and I don't push him away. I must admit it's nice to smile and laugh for a change especially now that the alcohol is taking effect.

I see Cole's scrutiny as he watches this man fuss over me. He's so angry and riddled with jealousy. He's panicking as if he's lost me. Well, good, maybe he did. He can't demand my love when his pregnant fiancé is upstairs. I lean into my new friend and tell him I am taking off; I am not feeling that great anyway.

I give Cole one last glance before I walk away. He mouths my name, hoping I'll wait to leave until after his song is over. I don't and I'm up and grabbing my wallet next to me, leaving my coat checked in the closet.

I'm not fast enough. Cole catches up with me outside. He lunges forward grabbing me by the wrist, spinning me around, and forcibly slamming me into the side of my coupe.

"Mya. Wait." He's angry and for a split second I surrender to him. I stare into his blue eyes hoping that he'll declare his love for me, tell me he's changed his mind, and we're going to run off into the sunset together.

"NO!" I scream in his face and with both hands try to shove him away.

"God dammit, put a coat on, it's cold out," He growls as he wraps his coat around my shoulders. It smells like him, a sweet mixture of his cologne and a smoldering campfire. He doesn't let me go and he holds me at arm's length trying to rub the cold out of my arms.

"I'm sorry things are going down like this, Mya. I'm sorry I fucked up. I want to die knowing that I've hurt you, but I can't— "

"What? You can't be with me Cole!!!" I scream so loudly my lungs pinch with pain, and I try to shove him away again.

"I already know that detail, Cole. You don't have to keep saying it out loud, Cole." I repeat his name like a sloppy drunk poking at his irritability. It doesn't work, he's a statue. I bang my fists into his chest again and again trying to release myself from his grasp. He stumbles backwards away from my blows and once my eyes land on his, I slap him. He drops his head, surrendering to my abuse.

The contact with his face bites my hand and tears well up in my eyes. He takes my hand to his lips and kisses the sting away. As much as I want to give in to the intensity of the moment, I can't. He can't.

"You can't keep doing this, Cole. You can't keep looking at me and touching me this way. It's too hard. Just let me go, please." I can't argue with him anymore; my heart is defeated. My arms are weak from trying to fight him off, but I'm adamant. He won't release me; he only grips me tighter. He kneads my arms between his hands as if I'll be gone forever if he lets go.

"Let. Go. Of. Me." I look him straight in the eye as I broadcast my sudden sobriety. My eyes are detached and empty, there's nothing left for him to see there. I'm not allowed to love him anymore.

He hesitates and struggles with his final move, unsure of what to do. But he does finally release me and when he does, he takes a desperate gasp of air as if he's having his last breath ripped out of his lungs. As if he just dropped me over a cliffs' ledge to my death. He hangs his head and his voice cracks in pure agony.

"Don't go, Mya. Please."

Free now, I turn away and get into my car.

I'm already gone.

17

Cole

Time is suspended.

She's gone.

I'm devastated. The pain is excruciating as I watch her taillights speed off and disappear around the bend.

The knot in my stomach breaches my throat and I release her name on a blood curdling scream. The ground beneath me quakes and I scream her name until

I have no air left. I hold out my hands and look down at them in disbelief. She was just in them moments ago; she was standing right here in front of me and now, she's gone.

I want to die seeing her so broken, knowing that I'm the cause of her pain and tears. Though she's slapped me before, this one was final, it was her last touch. And feeling Mya's delicate hand hit me, rather than touch me, is gut wrenching. I'm lifeless without her.

A fiery ball forms deep inside me, the fury is destructive. I'm rageful and I suddenly want to kill someone. Paige.

I should be happy with Mya but instead I feel murderous and I blame Paige. The laughs and memories she drew up fucked with my head. I was completely blinded by her return. I slept with her because it was Paige. It was routine and normal, it's what we did, it's what I knew. Now, a baby complicates matters; a baby will change everything. Mya understands that and it saddens me knowing how she knows it. I'm irrationally angry at her father for leaving her, but here I am doing the same thing.

"*Dammit. FUCK,*" I release a roar that draws the attention of many around me.

I turn around to face Styne's Tavern, fully intending to drown myself in booze. I start the walk back, numb from the realization that Mya is gone. Dustin appears, and next to him, Trisha. They stand just off the bottom step with their wide empathetic eyes taking in the full show. I stop abruptly, my jaw tightens and my hands ball into fists at my side. I glance down at Trisha's growing belly; and as murderous as I look, she doesn't flinch when I confront her. I put a hand in my brother's face communicating clearly not to fuck with me.

"How pregnant are you?"

"8 weeks." She doesn't hesitate to answer, nor does she elaborate. She looks relieved. I have just figured it out— the part of the story I'd been blinded to. She's a loyal friend so I know Mya is in the dark and she's kept this to herself. She can tell by my expression, red with wrath that my head seemed to explode with questions and a sudden need for confirmation.

***

I slowly ascend the stairs, one step at a time, feeling the full weight of my body with each step I take. I grip the railing hard to offer something to put my fist around. I look forward, my eyes never wavering.

I can't clear the thoughts racing through my mind. From one vision to the next it's a storm in my head— Paige's infidelity, Mya's timid smile telling me she's coming, visions of both grinding down on me, words like I hate you, I love you, let me go, and finally the sting of Mya's slap across my face sets me off. My thoughts only fuel me, intensifying the wrath I feel; my eyes glaze over and I'm no longer responsible for what is about to happen.

I slowly open the door to the apartment. I see candles lit and hear the sweet sound of an orchestra playing. Paige is taking a bath. I take heavy yet quiet steps toward the bathroom; I find the door slightly ajar. I reach out my hand and push it the rest of the way open and steam barrows out. The air smells of lilacs. Her robe is draped over the sink. She is naked. Her blonde hair had grown since her return; it's piled high on top of her head. Small beads of sweat pimple her forehead as she soaks in the hot bath. Her breasts peak just above the bubbles, drifting freely and swaying with the movement of the water. A sight which used to turn me on, now purely disgusts me. She tilts her head forward, her chin hitting the water as she takes a long sip of wine.

"Paige. We need to talk," I utter the words slowly, controlled, as to not lose my shit. Seeing a drink in her hand sickens me and I try to swallow the vomit that collects in my throat.

I can think of nothing more pleasing than pushing her head under the water and holding her there, depriving her of breath, waiting patiently until she drowns. The imaginary is so vivid I may have done it and wouldn't have known the difference between reality and the fantasy, but I walk away instead.

I sit on the couch and wait for her. The same couch I fucked her on weeks ago. Within a few moments she's out of the bath and dressed. She pulls her robe around her shoulders and approaches me flabbergasted.

"Colton, I thought you were playing tonight," she asks. I stand and tower over her. Her eyes widen as she looks up at me. She lifts her hands to lay them on my chest, but I grab her aggressively taking one of her wrists in one hand and with the other, I hold out a pregnancy test.

"Colton, what is the matter with you?"

Offended, she has the fucking audacity to be offended. I pull her by the arm and return her to the bathroom. She isn't struggling, but she's cursing at me, which I happily ignore. With my free hand, I pull down her pants, rip her underwear from her and kick the back of her knee forcing her ass down onto the toilet.

"Pee on the fucking stick, Paige." She grabs the test from my hand and removes it from its packaging. She isn't crying or even surprised at my demeanor or that I *appear* to have questions. I stand there and wait until she pisses on it, then I leave the bathroom and wait.

It's the longest three minutes of my life as I sit on the edge of the bed. My entire future with Mya is in there on the bathroom sink waiting to be read. I watch as Paige impatiently stands in front of the pregnancy test, fingers tapping at her sides. Soon, she picks it up and walks it over to me.

"See, you, fucking asshole, positive." She chucks the test at me and it lands at my feet. I pick it up to confirm the results for myself.

"That's fucking impossible, Paige. I haven't been with you for over a year."

"It takes just one time, Colton." She holds up her index finger as if I don't know what the fucking number one looks like. I know what day she's talking about. The day I've regretted from the moment it happened. I stand and pace the bedroom floor. She replaces me and sits down on the edge of the bed waiting for me to calm down.

"So, you're just going to leave me and the baby?" she asks sneeringly.

"NO, Paige, No."

I begin throwing everything in sight, like a toddler who's had a toy taken away. I rip the drawers out of the dresser. I send a lamp sailing into the wall, shattering it to pieces. I punch the window with the Grand Canyon crack in it and my knuckles erupt with blood and pain.

I move on to her nightstand kicking it over, the tiny drawer flies free spilling its contents at my feet. My heart stops. A tight ball forms in my throat and my eyes fill with tears. I bend over and pick up the sonogram picture, and under that, is a photocopied note. A threat, a copy of one sent to Mya, the one calling her a whore. An upsurge of vomit chokes me, if she has anything to do with Mya, I swear I'll kill her.

"What the fuck is this?" I ask but she's silent. *"What do you know Paige, why do you have this note?"*

With all corners of my world colliding, I'm unable to focus. I glance down at sonogram in my hand. The bitch won't talk but I must follow through with what already know, I need confirmation.

It has Paige's name and her date of birth, and a date of last week, an appointment date? I look at the tiny figure in the middle of the photo. Is that the baby? A small notation say's four months. My brain does a quick calculation. I scowl. Grabbing her by the throat I lift her to her feet. She never winces, she knows I won't really hurt her, not with her being pregnant. I release her throat and take a step back forcing my shoulder blades into the wall behind me, praying I don't do something stupid, like kill her.

"You're four months pregnant? I fucked you less than two months ago, which means you came back to me already pregnant. Are you still fucking him? Is that where you've been when you're not here." I stand there, again in disbelieve that I almost fell for this, another

future just ripped out from under me. *"It's not mine is it, Paige?"* She's frozen in place; she's failing at her attempt to distract me from the truth. *"I require a response!"* Still nothing.

"IS IT PAIGE?" The floor shakes under the explosion in my voice. I need her to say it out loud.

"You're the better man, Colton. He can't be a father, but you can."

That's all I needed, confirmation. The life I want and can have is now crystal clear.

I storm away from her and tear down the stairs two at a time. Paige calls after me realizing I'd just made myself very clear that we are through and that I want her out of my fucking life for good. I need to find Mya or someone who can get me to Mya.

I run into the bar completely forgetting that it's Friday night. The place is jammed with people and the music is loud. I am trying to find my breath when I'm immobilized at the sight of Mya hugging a man's arm. She's hanging off his jacket as if she's too drunk to stand on her own. Dustin and Trisha are gone, again, and Wyatt shrugs when I give him a questioning look. The PD does the same, they won't interfere. How much has she had to drink? I call for her above the crowd, but she doesn't respond and the man holding her taut to his side looks back at me nervously. I know him, he's familiar —why do I know him?

Paige finally catches up to me and she stands beside me as I watch Mya being half carried out of the bar.

"Oh my god, Sutton. That asshole."

I look at her in disbelieve of what I had just heard.

"Patrick Sutton?" She nods and I start a full sprint toward the door, knocking tables over and throwing chairs out of my way as I go. I catch up to them outside just as Mya's put into the back of a black jeep. I run towards it, but I can't catch them, and they speed off. I run a full sprint down the road chasing the jeep, screaming Mya's name.

She'd come back. She came back to the bar and it didn't matter why, she was there and now she's been taken, by the one person I tried to protect her from, because of the one person I once loved. Paige has a copy of the threatening note. She's fucking him. Fuck! I don't have time to find out what else she knows. I just need to know where he's taking Mya.

"Who the fuck is he, Paige?" my voice thunders across the parking lot. She knows I'm not playing her game anymore. Dustin comes barreling out of the Tavern, missing most of the steps on the way down.

I look at her again. *"Who is he Paige?"*

"Patrick Sutton, Cole, but sometimes he just goes by Sutton." She says. I pull my attention to Dustin who's overheard her as well and is already running towards his truck, but I scream for him to get to the PD anyway. I too tear out of the parking lot, fumbling with my phone before I'm able to connect a call to the PD.

"Get me everything you have on a Patrick Sutton and Peter Olden, an address, a hotel, an alias, whatever the fuck you can find on the names. You have five minutes."

***

I didn't expect him to be here. If you are going to kidnap someone you don't take them home. The PD called me back within three minutes with a *P. Sutton's* address. I took a chance and assumed it's my guy. At this point, I assume P. Sutton is also Mya's ex, aka Peter Olden.

I park down the road, pull my gun from the glove compartment, and prepare myself. I couldn't bare it if my love for her is what ends up getting her killed. As much as I don't want to numb myself to the situation, I can't be preoccupied that it's Mya who is in danger. This is what the Marines and police force trained me for. Departmentalize. I trust my training.

His black jeep is parked outside. I call the plates into the PD and spit the letters and numbers off realizing they are not the digits I memorized at Pins. I also tell them to send back up but to be quiet about it until I could get Mya out.

The house is a small, white, single story house, with black shutters and very little landscaping. I approach the house from the thick brush along the side of the neighbor's yard. I circle around back noting all the lights in the house are off. It's a small backyard so it takes no time at all to reach the broken screen door. That door is all that lies between the outside and the back porch. I enter the house, careful not to cause the screen door to creak. I stalk through, my gun drawn, clearing room by room waiting to be jumped, but no one comes.

There's no dog, no cat, there's hardly evidence that anyone lives here. I hear a moan and I look around the corner by the basement stairs. A small bedroom light serves as the answer I'm searching for.

I slowly approach the lit room and find Mya lying on top of the bed. There's a thin sheet under her but it does nothing to protect her from the dirt and disgust that covers the mattress. From here I can see one hand is tied to the bedpost and there's blood trickling down her cheek. Her skirt has been torn and her top is pulled up exposing her stomach. I turn away and wince, I'm going to kill him. With my gun drawn hoping I am not too late; I hold my breath.

I don't see him. I don't hear him. Mya's tossing her head from side to side as if she's trying to wake up and open her eyes. Oh baby, why'd you drink so much? My head falls back onto the wall, frustrated that I can't go to her yet. I need to find Olden first.

I hear laughter. Olden hangs up the phone from whomever he was talking to and is back in the room sitting down on the bed with her *"You were always so difficult love; this would've been over much sooner had you cooperated."*

He leans in closer to her and moans. She continues with slurred words as she tries to sit up, the ropes tug at her arms causing her to fall back down. He pulls himself up onto the bed and settles in next to her. Once he's sure the ropes are secure, he tugs at her skirt and slides one hand between the torn material. Her legs separate involuntarily as he slides his hand further up between them. *"You like that don't you hunny."* He lowers his face into her neck, inhaling her scent. Removing his hand, he then grabs her forcibly by the face, causing her lips to pucker and he brings his mouth to hers. That's when my first my warning shot goes off. Drunk or not, he's not fucking touching her anymore.

I am in a full sprint across the bedroom when my second shot is fired. I lunge my body into his, pushing him off the bed and away from her. I punch him once in the stomach and he fights back. I clip him with the handle of my gun and while he's down I kick him again.

172

He's up fast and yanks me up over the dresser and I tumble to the floor, losing my gun. I regain my footing, and dive at the sick fucker again. I quickly retrieve my gun from the floor, lift him up, and slam his back against the wall, pressing the end of the barrel deep into his temple.

I taste blood and I spit.

"I told you to back the fuck off." I pull the hammer back and press the gun in harder as I stare him in the eye. Peter quakes and pisses himself as I slowly move the gun to his mouth. *"I fucking told you I'd kill you."*

Two men stand next to me yelling my name; I heard them enter the house a while ago. Dave and Dustin stand beside me defensively as if I'm a ticking bomb ready to explode. With the end of my gun shoved in Peter's mouth, they urge me to take a beat. It's not worth killing him, they keep saying. Though the decision to release him should be an easy one, he took Mya and hurt her. For that I made a promise. I pop him in the throat, and he falls to the ground gasping for breath.

Dustin cuffs him and takes him out to the patrol car as Dave secures the bedroom. When I get close enough to Mya's side, I see she's completely tied to the bed. She wouldn't have been able to move even if she wanted to. Her cheek is swollen and bruised, and blood is smeared across her beautiful face.

"Mya. Baby?" She is unresponsive. I lift her upper body in my one arm as I undo the straps. *"I'm here, Mya."* Once free, I hold her limp face in my hand, trying to hold her chin still as it bobs from side to side. What the hell? I can barely make out her eyes as they roll in the back of her head. I lift her tiny frame into my arms and carry her outside. There's no time for tears or sadness or anything other than making sure she stays alive.

Outside, Dustin wants to call the ambulance, but I tell him no, I wasn't leaving her again. I put her in my truck, buckled her in, and speed to the hospital. The ride is quiet. Her shallow breathing is the only thing I'm focusing on in the silence.

"Stay with me, Mya." I whisper out loud into the darkness.

18

Mya

"Cole, I can walk." I say.

"Mya, don't argue."

"But Cole—."

"Mya, shut up." I surrender as Cole carries me from the wheelchair to the truck. Two days in the hospital after being drugged at Styne's. I had returned there after my argument with Cole. I didn't make it far down the

road before I turned around. I didn't feel well, really very sick actually, and I was not going to make it home. I also needed to tell him I was okay, that I didn't blame him, but when I got there, I couldn't find him. I remember being comforted by someone I recognized, but I was so dizzy I couldn't stand alone. I don't remember much after that. Cole has filled me in on most of what I don't remember. Though I can only imagine, he won't discuss in detail what happened, the condition he found me in, or Peter's intentions with me. Cole just assures me that he got to me in time.

I rest my head on the chilly window and Cole reaches over for my hand, gifting me with a reassuring squeeze. *"I'm okay,"* I say answering his silent question.

On the ride home, he fills me in on Peter's arrest. Though he hasn't confessed, he and Dustin assume Peter was the one making the threats, given that Paige had a copy of the note. She only knew him as Sutton. I feel free for the first time in months. Free from threats, from the Olden shooting, from my father's accident, then, when he finally uttered the words *it's not mine."* I've never been so elated. Now, I'm free to be with Cole completely, and how I've wanted to be with him since the beginning.

He picks me up out of the truck and carries me up the Tavern's front steps.

"I can walk, you know."

"Nope."

"Cole, I'm not an invalid." He continues to ignore my pleas.

Once inside front door, he finally put me on my feet. He pushes the door closed and turns to me. He wraps me in his arms, sets his chin on top of my head, and lets out the largest most satisfying sigh. One, I can only imagine he's been holding on to for weeks. He presses his lips into my forehead, kisses me, and leaves his lips to linger for a moment more.

"Come on, let's get you cleaned up." He says as we walk together upstairs to his apartment.

He turns the shower on and holds my hand as I step into the tub. He steps in behind me. The warm water rains over our bodies, washing away the pain from the last few weeks. For a minute he just holds me to his chest refusing to let go. He eventually takes the soapy cloth and drags it up and down my back. I stand motionless, staring and watching his face as he works his hands over my body. He sprinkles my skin with kisses after he's washed each area. His strong hands feel amazing against my skin again. He lightly runs his fingertips across my cheek, being gentle around the bruise.

"That was the last time you are ever going to be hit, you understand me." His eyes look pained with guilt.

"It doesn't hurt, Cole," I reassure him.

"Out you go." He orders, ignoring my forgiveness for the guilt I know he's carrying.

He pats me dry until every drop of water is absorbed. He pulls one of his baggy t-shirts over my head; the nightshirt smells like him. I stop his hands before he has a chance to take them off me. We both stand suspended as he searches my face questioning my next move.

I lift myself onto my toes. I let a low moan slip through my lips as I kiss his, sucking only a little on his bottom lip to send a message that I want him. My core is set alight when he responds. His thumb pulls on my bottom lip, opening my mouth as he brings his lips closer, his tongue darting out in search of mine. The warm welcoming pulse in my folds returns with a vengeance. Everything is forgotten and we are just here and now, free to be together.

I dip my fingertip between the towel and his skin and pull down and watch the towel fall to the floor. I return my gaze to his pained cautious eyes. He stands unmoving, his jaw line ticking, and his breathing is uneven. He's hesitant to allow what's coming, but I lower myself to my knees anyway. He lightly pushes the top of my head with his hand accepting and encouraging my intent. His need for my mouth just makes me hotter.

His cock grows as I lower myself down and eventually it stands at attention. I take the full thickness of him into my hand and hold the base of his cock in my other. I wet my lips and wrap them around his tip. Feeling his cock expand and pulse in my mouth sends warm sensations between my thighs. He lets out a groan which tells me he likes what I'm doing. His hands lay on the back of my head controlling the pace at which I take him. His thickness fills my mouth. I send him deep into the back of my throat and he groans a delicious sound. I withdraw, suck and lick the tip, pushing my tongue into the small slit. I send him down deeper into my throat and he releases another growl, this one more pronounced than the last.

I push down on his shaft and pull back up as my tongue circles and licks away a pearl of precum seeping out of his tip. I take him in again and the vibrations of my moans cause his muscles to tense. I know he's close. He holds my head in place with both hands as he thrusts a few times. I start to play with myself as he slowly fucks my face and suddenly on an exhale of my name, he finds his release. A band of his salty cum escapes into my mouth, I suck and lap at his tip and he watches.

***

"Good morning, beautiful." He stares at me with his head propped up on his hand, his elbow in the pillow. My face still swollen from sleep; I rub my eyes to clear my sight.

"What do you want to do today?" he asks like a happy schoolboy. I smile as many ideas come rushing to the forefront.

"What are you smiling at?" he asks as he runs his hand up and down my stomach, to my arm, my legs, and my neck. His touch feels so damn good. Its genuine and it keeps me grounded. He examines every inch of my body making sure he hasn't missed a spot.

"Take me downstairs," I mutter shyly under my breath.

"To the bar?" He quips.

"No stupid to your—room."

"Ohhh, I've wanted to bring you down there since the first time I met you. The day I pulled you over, I wanted to punish you. I wanted to bring you here and fuck the stubbornness right out of you—but—it's not my room."

I'm up and out of the bed before he can catch me. I glare at him for an explanation. His arms fly up in defense, laughing, and he explains that it's technically Dustin's room; that he just uses the gym down there. Dustin is wild and dominant and well somehow finds more satisfaction in that stuff than he does.

"But…if you want me to handcuff you again baby, I'll gladly do it." He quips and I join him back in bed. I

toss and turn looking at him questioningly trying to make sense of how that room is Dustin's.

"So...Trisha?"

"Yeah, probably." He responds with a shrug, tipping me over and landing on top of me. He brushes my lips with kisses testing my acceptance of him. And just like that our morning starts with catching up on missed time.

19

Cole

Several months later

"*Mya, I'm late. I got to go!*" I yell up the stairs to her as she finishes getting ready for work.

"*Fine…its fine. Trisha's coming to pick me up. I'll see you tonight. Cole.*" She hollers back.

It doesn't bother me that she didn't say she loves me. It's been a couple of months, but deep down the thought of Paige's pregnancy still makes Mya uneasy and she questions my love for her. Whether it is mine or not, how things played out took its toll on her. I love her, she's safe, we are together, and that's all that matters to me.

I pick up my wallet, keys, badge, and secure my weapon. I step out onto the porch and take in the Spring morning. I start the truck and look back to the door to see if she's coming. She's not and that's okay. It is quiet this morning on North Campbell Drive. I've been staying with her most of the time and staying at the apartment only on Friday nights.

"Shit," I stammer. I get out of the truck, walk back up to the front step yelling toward the back of the house.

"Russ, come on buddy." Our Russell Terrier comes running from behind the house wagging his tail.

"Get in there, buddy. Mommy will give you a treat."

I make a few calls to prepare for today.

I'm on patrol.

20

Mya

"*Trisha*." I snap my fingers meticulously at her to collect her attention.

"*Missouri Holdings is in today for a contract update and Snyder and Dolan are increasing their retainer. Do you know why?*"

"*All they said is that they had something they needed us to look into.*" She explains quietly, holding her hand over the phone's receiver, with a residual grin across her face. I roll my eyes; she's taking this sexy pregnancy body to a whole new level.

"I'm taking your car. I 'm going to the storage unit to pick up the files on Missouri. I'll be back in fifteen minutes." She waves me off, still blushing from whatever Dustin is uttering in her ear.

"Bitch, making me walk," I mutter annoyingly as I find her car parked at the far end of the lot. Being as pregnant as she is and eating as much as she does, she is under the impression that the extra walking will burn some extra calories. Um, No.

I start the car and speed off around the corner heading to the storage facility. Fifteen minutes is not a lot of time and I do not want to be late or unprepared for either meeting.

"Shit...shit...I don't have time for this!" I see a familiar sight of a police car pulling out behind me, the lights screaming and the siren wailing. *"Urgh,"* I pull over.

"Come on, come on," I utter impatiently. Then, in my rearview, I see the most perfect strut on two legs walking toward the car. My cheeks immediately crimson and I begin trembling. It's not a policeman. It's Cole, in a suit. I fly my head around looking behind me, looking to each side of the car. Where did he go? I am grinning like a foolish schoolgirl. Then he appears directly in front of my car, and out of my windshield, the most amazing sight, the epitome of *sex on legs*. His grin makes my entire body vibrate with pleasure and excitement. My

hands are shaking so badly I can't roll the window down, so he opens my door instead.

"Ma'am, I pulled you over because, once again You. Were. Speeding." He stresses the last three words independently because I was indeed speeding. I look around to see people gathering on the sidewalk. It is crowded with onlookers, my mother, Trisha and Dustin, Wyatt and many others.

He takes my hand to help me out of the car. My heels hit the ground and the Spring air warm my bare legs and sends my dress sailing. He kneels in front of me and pulls out a tiny black velvet box. I look down at him, my eyes now blind with tears.

"Mya, my life began again after meeting you. Much like today you sped into my life and put a heartbeat inside of me again. My heart now belongs to you. Our lives intertwine perfectly, and I'll love you forever, Mya. Will you marry me?"

I'm rendered speechless, tears come full stream down my cheeks. *"Tell me I'm wrong baby"* He quickly and quietly continues, worrying because I've yet to say something.

"You're not wrong, Cole. Yes. I'll marry you, a thousand times yes!"

He stands and slips a diamond ring on my finger. The crowd breaks into an applause and cheers as he lifts me into the air. Slowing his movements, he pulls me into his chest and kisses my forehead.

***

"We should have taken the day off," he quips and we both burst into laughter.

"I just get engaged and now I have to go back to work and be expected to focus." I whine, watching as the crowd disperses.

"Such is life, baby." He kisses me again, whacking me on the butt and struts back to his patrol car, wiggling his ass a little for my entertainment. He's no match for the deliriously happy state he's leaving me in. He mouths the words *"slow down"* to me on a grin before he pulls away. I gaze down at my ring as I watch my fiancé drive away.

21

Cole

"Let me talk to him, five minutes, Pop. It's all I need."

The last thing I want on the same day I propose to Mya is to see Peter Olden's face, but I can't avoid it. His hearing was rescheduled this morning and it's my last chance for answers before he's taken away. I am requesting, well demanding, five minutes with him. As cops we know why he did what he did. He was a drunk kid who rented a car as P. Sutton. He intended to get put away and did so for five years for assault, and just like that Sutton disappears and Olden is behind bars. He only met Mya once he got out of jail. We know that he shot his mother accidentally, as he was trying to scare Mya. We know that he had a friend drug Mya and lure her out of the bar for his benefit, but now as Mya's fiancé, I have a few more questions.

"You have five minutes, Cole." Pop gives me a stern eye above his glasses before he opens the interrogation room.

I walk in and sit down in front of him. Olden is cuffed to the table and he attempts to match the anger in my face. He can't, he is no match for me.

"Why?" That one word is laden with questions and he knows exactly what information I am looking for.

"How does it end for you Peter, huh? Ten to fifteen years for causing the pile up, for murder, for attempted murder, for stalking Mya. I asked you a fucking question!" I scream in his face and mirror my anger with a fist to the table.

He sits quietly, smug, and staring at his cuffed hands, fumbling with the cuff of his shirt.

"Why Mya?" I ask again, but it didn't matter the answer. I'm going to beat the shit out of him, regardless. Then he speaks.

"You mean, Paige, don't you? Why did I fuck your fiancé?" It's off topic, but he asks it with a smile.

"I asked about Mya, you asshole. Why the pictures, why the threats? She didn't know it was you at the house, you were supposed to be long gone." I'm spitting nails. I want to kill him. My screams catch the attention of the officers outside.

"Easy. Target." He mouths the words slowly on a smirk. *After all this time, my girl still has some paranoia issues, doesn't she Mr. Styne?"*

"DON'T!" I roar. *"She's not yours?"* I pop him in the face, knocking him out cold. I'm pulled out of the room by the Dustin and Dave before I can take another hit. I shake myself free and stalk off to Cap's office. Within minutes after assessing my damage he storms into the office.

"Pretty sure you broke his face, Cole."

"Good."

***

Playing tonight is different, not only am I struggling because my hand hurts from punching Peter, but because I'm happy, finally. Mya and I are together. Dustin and Trisha have taken over the apartment upstairs as they prepare for the baby and Mya said yes today.

It's not long into my set before she walks in. She's beautiful, grinning with her full mouth and women crowd her to gawk at her ring. I stand behind my guitar watching her every move and now I'm distracted as fuck seeing she wore those boots again. There is a bounce in her step that I've not seen in a long time. She's happy, in love, and free to be with—me. She glances up to the stage and I sing as I always do, directly to her, and everything else fades away and we are the only two left in the room. My heart's pounding. The distance between us is too great, I want to touch her, carry her away, and make love to her.

She sits proudly on her barstool sipping her wine. Wyatt gives me a nod confirming that it's the only drink she'll have tonight since she's heading out to her mother's cottage in a few hours.

The dance floor is buzzing, and everyone is having a fucking great time. Mya's dancing and singing along to my songs. I've been on stage all night; I haven't heard her sweet voice yet.

It's a quarter to eleven when Mya eyes me and waves goodbye. I mouth *I love you* to her and she holds her hand to her chest and smiles. In a blink, she's gone.

***

191

Her mother's cottage is tricky to find, but when I do, I sneak in later than I expected to. I sleep in the den, so I wouldn't wake anyone up.

The next morning, I find Mya and her mother out in the gardens filling their wicker baskets with flowers. She is right, this cottage and property is breathtakingly beautiful. I stand at the back door drinking my coffee, when her brother Brody enters the kitchen.

"Come on, man, we have work to do." He pats me on the back and hands me the list of repairs that need to be made around the house.

We set out to the shed for some tools and he and I spend the morning fixing leaky sinks and patching the holes in the walls where her mother had removed artwork. Then we hang new, mother approved, pre-selected, pictures frames in their place. I change the oil their mother's car while Brody replaces a headlight, the list went on and on. Mya makes Brody and I lunch, and she kisses my cheek thanking me for helping her brother.

We steal a few hours alone at the overhang which sits at the back of the property. Our fingers intertwine freely as we take in the sights and smells of Spring. Her body presses on my body and our breathing aligns. I couldn't have asked for a better future than the one I have planned with Mya. In subtle conversation, I tell her I must head home until tomorrow night to help Dave with a case.

She assures me, as if I am the one who needs comforting, that with Peter in jail and her mother and Brody around she'll be fine.

The day passes and dinner is over. I watch Mya and her mother in the kitchen as they chat and giggle over proposed wedding plans.

"Mya, I have to head back to Lorry Springs until tomorrow night. Clear a few things up before Monday morning," I tell her as I gather my things together. I say it more for her mother's benefit than hers, since she already knew my plans. She and her mother both turn and wave goodbye as though I am interrupting their intense discussion over flowers and venues. I find Brody in the living room watching the game. *"Text me the score man."* I punch him playfully in the arm and he waves goodbye in between forks full of pie.

***

Back at the station, I impatiently pace the floor so frantically the carpet is appearing worn from my steps.

"Carol, where is he?" My father takes his sweet time getting his ass back here with the details of Paige's whereabouts.

She hasn't been seen since the night Olden assaulted Mya. Dustin and Dave have been working on the case quietly as to not alarm Mya or even Trisha in her delicate condition. I pulled Mya's protective detail when we locked Olden up for kidnapping and sexual assault, we added a few years once we positively identified him as the drunk driver that killed her stepdad. I rested easy, for a while; I did. But when a new message, a threat, came to Mya's place, I immediately went back on guard. I had already pulled her detail, so reinstating them would have caused her alarm. Luckily, I intercepted the note and she never laid eyes on the goddamn thing. All it said was

HOMEWRECKER.

That one word would have splintered Mya, it would have broken her heart. She would have blamed herself for this baby growing up without a father, me or Peter, it didn't matter, she'd somehow find herself at fault. I'll die before I let anyone hurt her again. The message must've been from Paige, who else? I never thought she would stoop this low. My pacing ceases when Pop comes swinging through his office door.

"So?" I ask curtly.

"We don't know, Cole, we just don't know where she is." I run my fingers through and yank at my hair. Fuck. I've tried to call her, she doesn't answer. It's the only time in the last several months I want to get in touch with Paige. Captain assures me that the deputies have staked out her apartment, the Tavern, the doctor's office, and the hospitals. There's just no sign of her. She must be

eight or nine months pregnant by now. I'm extremely frustrated, how the fuck can we miss an 8-month pregnant woman.

With Mya at her mother's, I can only help until I return to Somerset tomorrow night. I won't leave her alone without me for too long.

"I'm running home to let Russ out and feed him," I tell my father as I exit his office.

"I'll be back in an hour."

***

I gather up a few things for our dog, feed him his favorite leftovers. *"Shh, don't tell Mommy,"* I say quietly patting him on the head. He wags his tail and jumps up licking my face. *"Eh...Russ."* I let him outside and throw a ball with him a few times to tire him out. I settle him in for the remainder of the evening. *"I'll be back in a while, buddy,"* I say, rubbing his tummy and playing a quick game of tug of war with his chew toy.

***

The weekend offers no leads. My desperate attempt to find Paige before I had to go back to Somerset were unsuccessful. There's no sign of her. Although I'd love to think she took off, the note she left screams vengeance. Paige is angry and hurt and she's looking for revenge.

There's nothing left for me to do right now. I miss Mya, I've been away from her too long. Brody and I have a few more things to check off the to-do list before we call it quits. His return has been a nice excuse to leave Lorry Springs for a few days, but one more night in Somerset and I'll have to bring her back home.

***

One song plays and then another as I sit here idle in traffic. I inch the car forward little by little, getting closer to the action every few minutes.

"Jesus. Shit, that looks really bad," I mutter to myself, eyeing a sea of red and blue lights up ahead. I look to the right and see the yellow "hidden drive" road sign. I look straight between the emergency vehicles and I see the bend in the road.

"Oh, no, no no…" I pull the truck over and rifle through my memory for Mya's description of where her mother lives. It was hard to tell in the dark, I'd only been out here this one time.

My shaking frame validates what I already know. I get out of the truck and walk only a few steps before I see a jeep off the road. It's rolled over with all the windows blown out. Its condition tells me it rolled a few times before finally landing on its roof. I pick up the pace and jog closer to the jeep. I start reading the letters and numbers, recognizing them as the plates I memorized from Pins. Panic sets in. I'm scoping the scene for any evidence, any confirmation of what I have yet to articulate.

"Hey, where's the driver of the jeep?" I shout to a first responder.

He points with his clipboard to the ambulance across the street. A black bag lays extended on a stretcher. It's zipped halfway up leaving the face exposed. It's a woman, with a protruding stomach. My heart sinks as I slowly walk toward the stretcher. I'm close enough now, I can see her face. It's Paige. She's dead. My heart aches. I didn't expect to feel this way—the baby. Before I finish unzipping the bag to take in the full sight of my dead ex fiancé, I hear a familiar voice heading in my direction.

"Cole?"

"Dave? What the fuck is Lorry Springs PD doing here?"

"Cole. The accident. It's just too big for Somerset." Too big? He put his hand to my chest trying to hinder my steps. My breathing hitches, and my heart literally stops beating when I see the sadness, sympathy, and terror painted on his face.

I already know what he's going to say, but he mustn't say it. I circle around and push past him. I hear him shouting after me as my eyes dart from vehicle to vehicle in search of her car.

"Cole, wait man, don't."

I start to sprint and push my way through everyone standing in my way. The police cars, fire vehicles, and ambulances have barricaded her car from onlookers.

"No. *NO! Mya*??? I scream. I'm out of breath, I can't breathe.

Pop turns toward me. *"Dustin, goddammit, I thought I told you not to call him."*

He and Dustin catch me by the shoulders, holding me back from proceeding any further.

"Mya, MYA!!" I scream her name again and again. My worst fears are suffocating me, and it takes all I have, to get her name out.

"Cole. Don't son." It's all they can do to hold me back and two more deputies join their efforts.

"That's her car Dad. FUCK! MYA!!!!" I can't hear her. I look up at my father then at Dustin. My terrified eyes dart rapidly between them wordlessly asking them questions, so many questions.

"Why is she not responding to me?" I'm finally able to articulate one as I see a fireman replacing the tools and saws, they used to extract her from the car.

"No, no, no...Mya." I collapse and fall to my knees.

I sob as I watch the EMTs and firemen pull her from the vehicle. She's bloodied and bruised. She's unconscious and her lifeless body dangles from the fireman's arms as he puts her onto the backboard. An EMT supports her head as another places an oxygen mask over her face. The painful sight playing out in front of me is ripping the heart from my chest. The pain is excruciating. I just lost everything; the one great thing left in my life is gone. This emptiness is too much. A life without Mya, it's unbearable. I punch the pavement and let out a thunderous cry. My fist explodes with pain.

"Cole, Calm down. She's alive, she's alive." I settle immediately from the words my father is saying. I stare blankly and wait for him to clarify. I wait for his next words, but he's too quiet for too long. I rise to my feet and start to bolt.

"Let me see her, let me go to her." I'm stopped again by the swarm of LSPD officers who refuse to let me get any closer.

"You can't Cole, they're working on her." Dave rests his hand on my shoulder. I push past him and throw my

fist into a patrol car window; my goddamn hand explodes with blood and pain again.

"Cole, dammit son, there's nothing you can do right now other than go to the hospital and wait." Pop dictates the order to me.

"It's my fault. I pulled her detail. I was supposed to be with her." I howl angrily as I stare at Paige's dead body. I knew she is in danger. I thought I could protect her. My eyes fill with tears as I watch Mya be taken away in the ambulance.

It's my fault.

I pulled her detail.

22

Mya

"I hear you, Cole. I hear you. I wasn't speeding, I promise."

My words are clear in my head, but my lips won't move, and I have no voice to say them with. My eyes squint open just enough to see lights, a lot of lights. My body is twisted and trapped under the steering wheel. I'm disoriented. I can taste dirt in my mouth and feel the shards of glass in my cheek.

It burns.

I hear a chainsaw. Sparks fly above me like beautiful fireworks on the Fourth of July.

The screeching sound of metal on metal is giving me a headache. The voices yelling and screaming above me aren't helping.

I can barely make him out in the distance as they pull me from the car, but I can hear him crying my name.

I'm alive, please stop fussing over me. I try to open my eyes a little more, but I can't.

The firm thrusts on my chest hurt. The air being forced into my mouth is unpleasant, and I want to cough but I can't. I taste blood. I hurt all over and what strength I have left is subsiding. I am so cold. I'm so tired.

Then everything goes black.

23

Cole

Two Weeks Later

"She won't wake up, Dad." It's the first time in my life that I let myself just lose control like a child would. My head falls heavily into my hands and I sob, thinking the worst but praying for the best. I try to remember the last thing I said to her. I can't remember. She can't die, but my only coping mechanism is to assume she will.

"Tell me I'm wrong, Pop. Tell me she won't die." He says nothing. He just sits beside me with his arm draped over my back. He's calm; he's being strong for me. He

is just a father comforting his son in his desperate time of need.

Mya has been unconscious since they pulled her from the car. That was two weeks ago. The blow to her head when her car was hit head on caused swelling and bleeding on her brain. The doctors say that it'll take time for her to heal. Machines mostly take care of her now, all I can do is sit and wait for her to come back to me.

24

Mya

I can feel the heat of his hand wrapped around mine. I feel his lips pressing into my fingertips. I know you're here, Cole. I just can't tell you.

I hear music, it's like angels singing.

"Wake up, Mya. Please, I need to see you." I can tell from his voice he's scared. I feel his teardrops fall and roll down my hand. It tickles.

"Baby, please." He's begging, he's losing faith. How long have I been here? He releases my hand and I feel the bed sink down.

My mother. She sits beside me moving the loose hairs off my face. I'm so tired mom. I'm so tired. I've lost all track of time.

I hear Cole greet the doctor and they prepare to hear an update on my condition.

"Since the last scan, the brain swelling has gone down tremendously and the bleeding has stopped finally. The new x-ray's show both bones have healed. We still just have to wait for her to wake up."

My mother takes my hand and kisses it.

"You're going to be okay, Mya," She whimpers.

Mom?

Brody?

Cole?

He's breathing steadily. He's sleeping.

Hello?

The room is quiet.

Everything is quiet.

Beep…Beep…Beep.

"Cole."

25

Cole

I've been here for weeks, working only when I know Mya's mother and Brody are at the hospital. I will not leave her alone again. The indescribable guilt I carry is unbearable.

She was in trouble again. I thought I could protect her on my own. Paige saw that opportunity, that weakness, and tried to take her from me. Peter's still in prison. He's tried to off himself twice since his attorney told him that both Paige and his baby are dead.

I take her hand and hold it in mine, and as I always do, I press my lips into her fingertips. *"I love you, Mya. Please wake up."* I mean the words as deeply as ever, but I have run out of tears. Every day is the same, I sit in this chair with my head resting on the side of the bed. Sometimes I bring the guitar and strum cords until my fingers are numb.

When I'm here, her hand is in mine and I don't let it go. Touching her and feeling her warmth is the only thing that confirms she's alive, and she'll eventually come back to me. The same low beeps and puffs of air which keep her stable, put me to sleep.

"Cole."

I'm startled awake. The hair in my ears vibrate with the residual sound of my name being spoken. I glace at the clock, it's 2:00 am. I release her hand and stand to stretch my back and legs. I look at her stats on the monitors and note that the nurses have already been in to change her IV bags.

"Cole."

The hair on my arms spring to life as my ears ring again. That sweet, delicate voice breathes life in me. Fearing I'll wake up from a dream, that this moment isn't real, I let my arms fall to my side. I stand still, quiet, and wait.

"Cole."

I knew it! My heart explodes. I jump to her side, grab her hand and begin stroking her forehead.

"Mya baby. Mya...open your eyes." I laugh, I cry, but my voice won't go above a whisper as I try to yell for the nurse. I reach over pressing Mya's call button instead.

My eyes are on her, praying hard she'll say my name again. But nothing. She's quiet and still again as the nurse checks her vitals.

"She's definitely awake," she says chuckling. *"Her vitals jumped just a few moments ago. Keep talking to her."*

"You're a stubborn stubborn woman, Mya Dylan. Please, baby...please wake up." I pull on my hand to wipe my brow, but I feel resistance. I stare down at her hand, I refuse to blink until I see her move again.

"Mya?" Her fingertips start moving.

"Keep talking, keep talking," the nurse exclaims as she stirs excitedly around the room, calling for the doctor.

"Mya...baby, open your eyes. I want to see you." I am tearful, fueled with excitement that this could be the moment I look into her beautiful green eyes again.

"Come on baby…come back to me." Her eyelids flutter open and I see them. Her big, beautiful, full green eyes, full of love, full of life.

"Oh my god, baby." I lift her hand to my lips and kiss her, refusing to detach the two. Her eyes grow wider as she looks around the room. I stroke her head and tell her everything will be okay and that she is safe.

The doctor comes around to her bedside. He shines his light in her eyes to inspect her reflexes.

"Everything looks good. Mya." He talks slowly and loudly to her, his words pronounced trying to keep her alert. *"Mya. It's Dr. Steinman at Lorry Springs General Hospital. Can you hear me, can you say something?"*

She slowly turns her head in my direction, her eyes finding mine, she reaches up and grabs her diamond ring that dangles from my neck and she whispers.

"I love you."

COLE

Two Months Later

"Come here," I say calmly, reaching out for her.

I take her into my arms and try as I always do to comfort her after we argue. But this time something is different. She's not pushing me away, we aren't screaming at each other, and she hasn't kicked me out, yet.

It's a breakthrough.

Since Mya came home from the hospital, she's been irritable and depressed. We argue over everything, mostly over Paige. The thought of the baby and Paige dying in the accident, broke her. It's irrational but she thinks I'm heartbroken over loosing Paige. I swore to her I wouldn't give up on her even after she called the wedding off. Her therapist said she just needed time to readjust to her life. Someone tried to kill her, and that someone, I used to love, and whom she thought, for a long time, was pregnant with my baby. It'll take time. She's been through so much.

"Tell me baby, please open up to me."

212

It's the closest I've come in weeks to getting through to her. Her face falls into her hands. She begins sobbing and pushes herself out of my embrace.

"It's Paige, it's work, it's Brody, it's my mom, it's you, Cole, it me, the fucked up me, it's just everything."

It's the first time since she's been home that she's on the brink of final destruction. I stand there. I tread lightly, careful not to make a wrong move, or say the wrong thing. I give her space, trying not to ruin this moment of clarity she's having. I watch as she's coming undone, and I wait, impatiently for her permission to come closer.

"I'm sorry you're going through all of this Mya. I want to be here for you, I do. If you'll let me." I choose my words carefully. They are the same ones I've said many times before, before they backfire.

"Cole, when I said I didn't want to marry you. I meant, "not right now, not…ever. I love you. I feel like you are just trying to get the normal Mya back, the one before the accident. What if I can't be that Mya for you?"

"There she is. Finally, baby," I release my breath. My heart breaks hearing her consider that she knows my feelings, my thoughts, or what I want. I push my shoulders off the wall and approach her. I wrap my entire frame around her body and hold her as tight to my chest. Her tiny arms wrap around me as she sobs, freely

and uncontrollably. I kiss the top of her head, her peach shampoo bringing all my senses back to life.

When she finally calms enough, I take her face between my hands and bring her lips to mine. Her eyes, deep and green which were suffering are now free again. Mine full of love, comfort and support that she knows she can bury herself into. I gently brush my lips against hers, testing her tolerance of me. She doesn't push me away, and that's a good sign, so I make my move.

I kiss her tenderly, waiting for her to grant me access. She does, and I love on her, touch her and make sweet love to her until we are Cole and Mya again.

MYA

I'm startled awake, when I hear Russ barking. I take in my surroundings and remember it's Friday night. Cole has already left for Styne's.

By the time I get there, the place is in full swing. I head up the flight of wooden stairs to the wrap around porch when I hear a familiar squeal.

"Yeah Bitch…you came?" Trisha waddles over to me.

"Ya know, you're going to be a mother soon, you have to stop using 'uh-oh' words." I lift my fingers into air quotes.

"Yeah, yeah, when I push this kid out…I'll change my language until then, fuck that. She stresses the *uh-oh'* word and I roll my eyes.

"I want to see Cole." I say, rolling my eyes at her.

The place is wild, the music is loud, Cole is solo tonight. I watch as his body sways and bounces to the rhythm. He looks delicious in his faded jeans and his cowboy hat casting that mysterious shadow across his face that I love so much.

He hasn't spotted me yet, but I am enjoying the view. Also checking out the view, is a red haired, smoky eye,

215

twenty-something who approaches me from behind the bar. Wyatt looks at me and laughs as he makes goo-goo eyes at the new bartender. Dirty old man.

"Hi, Mya, right?" She squeals as annoyingly as Trisha does. She hasn't taken her eyes off Cole and I am starting to get fucking pissed about it.

"A beer, please." She literally has the audacity to open and hand me a beer, while never taking her eyes off Cole. He looks up and finds me sitting in front of her.

"Name's, Brooke. You're one lucky girl." Finally, some validation; she knows he's taken.

I turn to watch Cole who's looking extremely twitchy. He's singing is disciplined and amazing. He's eyes are mostly fixed on mine. He glances over to the new bartender every so often, he fancies her or she him, I suppose we'll find out. I remain at the bar until his song is over and he soon joins me.

"Cole, want a drink?" Brooke askes him, her gross tits pool out of her corset as she leans over the bar. I just about burst into laughter spitting out my beer as I watch him become more and more uncomfortable with her presence.

"Whiskey," he replies, never taking his eyes off me.

"Oh, good boy, you show restraint, impressive." I'm sarcastic and try to hide my smirk.

"Baby, you have no idea. You've met Brooke?" He asks. His eyes are dark and wild.

"I have, and her friends too." I reply, cupping my breasts in my hands and giving them a tender squeeze.

"Come here." He growls. And in a shot, he sweeps me away from the bar, into the hallway where he first touched me, and like he did then, he pushes me up against the wall. With one arm, he pulls my leg up over his hip and pushes his erection into my center showing me just how hard he is. His hand slides up underneath my skirt, his fingers glide swiftly across my clit. I'm panting, breathing heavily, under his expert touch. It feels so good to be back in his arms.

"I love you." It is more than just a statement or a declaration. He's begging, hoping I'll really hear him and understand his words.

"I love you too." I reply as he lifts me up into his arms. My legs find their own way over his hips and I motion for him to take me downstairs.

For the first time and for the next two hours, Cole uses my body for his own pleasure. I know he loves me, and he won't hurt me, that notion has long passed. But for a little while, we become two different people, free, with no judgements. He can tie me up, penetrate me with objects and take away all my senses, I'm even more turned on, and when I beg him to stop, he only thrusts his cock that much harder into me. It's a fierce recurring scene that plays out until we are both exhausted and hung over from pure sexual ecstasy.

The phone rings. It's Dustin. I find it comical as I listen to Cole's excuses as to why we are down here, but it doesn't matter, Dustin is calling for another reason.

"It's time, Aunt Mya" Cole excitedly mumbles the words to me, grinning wide as he disconnects the call.

COLE

"Hi baby." I kiss my girl hello when she comes back to the waiting room. We hold each other's hands waiting for the news.

"You're shaking," I observe, bringing her hand to my lips for a supportive kiss.

"I'm just excited. It's a baby Cole...Trisha and Dustin with a baby." Her eyes are wide, full of life, and exhilaration. It is the perfect time. I turn to her, take her engagement ring out of my breast pocket, the one she threw at me weeks ago after a fight.

"Baby, we never have to walk down the aisle. You never have to become Mrs. Styne. But I love you and you are and will always be mine. Please---" my declaration of love is interrupted when she hurdles herself at me, entangling her body in my arms.

"This is way better than the first time I proposed." I quip.

"Shut up. " She laughs.

We sit for an hour more holding each other, waiting, when Dustin finally appears with an update.

"It's a BOY!!!" Dustin exclaims loudly into the waiting room. Mya packs up her bag, quicker than shit, and sprints down the hallway leaving my brother and I to a moment alone.

"Congratulations brother." I pull him in for a hug.

***

We sit together and melt over this amazing little bundle that just arrived. Trisha looks amazing and my brother couldn't be a happier new dad. Mya looks like an angel with a baby in her arms. I watch her as she embraces such a delicate thing, she's a natural and it only makes me fall in love with her more.

After an hour or so, the nurse takes the baby to the nursey. Mya and I decide to head home and let Trisha rest. We say our goodbyes and Dustin walks us out.

I give my girl the tightest embrace as if to tell her all that is in my heart. Before I leave myself, Dustin wants to check on his son again. I walk with him to the nursery. We gaze through the glass window to all the babies that lay there.

"There he is," Dustin points proudly.

"He looks just like you, brother." I observe.

We stare and gawk at the babies all snuggled in their blankets, like the goofy dorky new dad and uncle we are.

A man and woman join us at the window, rivaling Dustin and my gawking with their own. They look over to Dustin and asks which one is his. Dustin points proudly to his son. The couple does the same and the appropriate number of "oos" and "ahhs" are exchanged.

"Look hunny, she's still here?" the woman says to her husband, pointing to a baby in the back.

"Someone will take her soon, I'm sure of it," he replies, wrapping his arm around her. He turns to see mine and by brother's questioning look.

"The baby in the back is a little girl. She's been here awhile, if not longer than we have. Our little one was premature, but not her. It's just no one has claimed her."

"What about the woman who gave birth to her?" I didn't mean for it to come out as crass as it did; I thought it is an honest question.

"The mother died in a horrific car accident outside Somerset." The woman forces through an exhale, bringing her hand to her chest. *"The poor girl doesn't have a mother."* She adds.

"When they brought the mother into the morgue, the baby had been expelled, but she was still alive. The EMS

hadn't noticed it at the scene or maybe it hadn't happened yet, no one knows for sure. But they found the poor baby in the body bag between her mother's legs when they got here. Can you just imagine."

The woman has said enough, and Dustin's arm come up and rests on my shoulder. My face pales and my heart stalls, it's beating so slowly I swear it has stopped. The realization pulls the air from my lungs, weakens my knees and makes me want to throw up. I look at Dustin who mirrors my absence for words. His eyes say it all. I turn and walk away.

Paige's baby is alive.

MYA

I expected to see him home before me since I had to stop at the office first. I walk in and find him at the kitchen table. His face is red, and he is sweating. My stomach starts turning, I have a feeling whatever he's about to tell me is not going to be good. I slowly approach where he is seated and lay my hand on his back.

"Cole, you okay?" I ask softly, and without looking up, without a preface to his delivery, he just goes right for the jugular.

"It's Paige."

I don't respond. I make no acknowledgement that he just said that woman's name. The woman who tried to kill me. I was in a fucking coma because of that woman. If I had never heard her name again it would have been too soon. I remove my embrace from his shoulder, turn away and take myself to the kitchen. With my back to him, I pull a wine glass down from the cabinet. I have nothing to say about that woman.

"Mya…" he starts, but I interrupt. I won't let him talk to me about her.

"Cole, I don't want to hear anything there is to hear about that woman. She ruined—."

Another goddamn glass falls from my hand, shattering to pieces on the floor. I lose all feeling in my body. She?

My body and soul separate, I'm lightheaded, I feel as though I'm hovering above the situation. I must be. I can't deal with this. The only coping mechanism I have left is to leave.

The air in the room is thick, it suffocates me. My eyes are blind by the steady flow of tears that are forming without permission. My heart starts pounding, my hands become shaky and I turn to face him. He is already there, standing beside me, attempting to hold me still. I lift my eyes to his and let the tears fall. His face tells me all I need to know. His voice pleading with me.

"I saw her Mya. She's alone. She has no one.

EPILOGE

Eight Years Later

Vivian Marie leave your little brother alone, come on in, it's dinner time." I yell from the cottage windows which overlook the field just behind the gardens. Cole, I and the kids spend most of the summers here after my mother passed away. My mother left her beautiful retirement cottage to both Brody and me. Brody comes with his wife and daughter periodically throughout the year.

"Vivian and Jackson, it is time for supper." Cole yells again to them. *"Listen to your mother."*

I finish setting the table when Cole wanders in, grabbing me by the waist, and whispering in my ear. *"I want to see you tonight."* He makes me blush every time he says that to me. I fist bump his chest and his retort, a crack to my ass. He brings his lips to mine for a kiss which rivals any other we've shared.

I sit with my family eating dinner and while the kids chatter on with their dad, I reminisce over my glass of wine.

Cole did take me to see Paige's baby that next afternoon. The hospital had tried calling Cole several times after the accident. Paige had an old phone number down as her emergency contact and they assumed he was the baby's father. The hospital stayed quiet about Vivian surviving the accident mostly because she was expelled from Paige's body which brought on several medical complications.

I watched Cole's face that day as we stood listening to the doctor. He held my hand so tightly. Did he not know me at all? Did he not know how much I loved him, my future was with him and if he and I could make that little life better, I owed it to him, to try.

When I saw the baby for myself, there was no question.   The resentment I held on to with Paige dissolved when I held her baby for the first time. Her tiny toes and fingers. Her wide yawn and delicate squeal at the end, melted my heart and I fell in love with her.

She's a strong little girl to have survived such a horrific car accident. She isn't Cole's blood and she isn't mine but after the adoption went through, she was ours. A baby does change everything.

A year after we adopted Vivian, Cole and I became pregnant with a baby of our own. Jackson arrived and he's a spitting image of his father. Someday, Vivian will learn of her adoption, of her mother, and Cole will be sure she knows the good parts of Paige. But for now, love, life, and family are all that matter in the end.

Tell me I'm Wrong.

www.ingramcontent.com/pod-product-compliance
Lightning Source LLC
Chambersburg PA
CBHW071528110726
47908CB00003B/990